A GATHERING OF FLOWERS

Stories About Being Young in America

Edited by Joyce Carol Thomas

HarperTrophy
A Division of HarperCollinsPublishers

"Twisters and Shouters" is excerpted from *Tripmaster Monkey: His Fake Book* by Maxine Hong Kingston. Reprinted by permission of Alfred A. Knopf, Inc.

All other stories used by permission of the authors.

Typography by Joyce Hopkins

Library of Congress Cataloging-in-Publication Data
A gathering of flowers: stories about being young in America / edited by Joyce
  Carol Thomas.
      p.   cm.
    Summary: A collection of eleven short stories depicting what it is like to be
young in America, exploring such diverse cultures as urban San Francisco, a
Chippewa Indian reservation, and a Latino barrio in Chicago.
    ISBN 0-06-026173-0. — ISBN 0-06-026174-9 (lib. bdg.)
    ISBN 0-06-447082-2 (pbk.)
    1. Short stories, American. [1. Short stories.] I. Thomas, Joyce Carol.
PZ5.G3165   1990   90-4043
[Fic.]—dc20   CIP
                                                                             AC

For Maria Pecot, with love

ACKNOWLEDGMENTS

I thank my gentle, brave editor, Joanna Cotler, for insisting on this book, and assistant editor Susan Hill for her fine work.

I thank my wonderful agent, Mitch Douglas.

I thank the poet Myra Cohn Livingston for helping me remember the original meaning of the word "anthology," from which I named this collection.

I thank the gathering of writers included here, who answered my request for stories in the generous spirit of creativity and cooperation.

CONTENTS

INTRODUCTION

A statistician a while back wrote that "Everybody on this planet is at least a twenty-second cousin to everybody else." I interpret that to mean that a Hawaiian man is kin to a Polish woman on the other side of the world and that a Japanese girl is cousin to a South African boy. How much closer then are we all, living as we do in close proximity in these United States? Nations within a nation.

When I began to think about assembling this collection of short stories about being young in America, I wanted the fiction choices to include stories about Anglos, stories about Hispanics, stories about Asians, Native Americans, and African Americans. I wanted to put together a sampling of the rich colors and voices that make up today's America.

I had been fascinated by the possibility of a book like this for a long time. I found all the more reason for calling together this collection when I discovered that a majority of present-day elementary and secondary school students in many California cities are from ethnic groups other than white American. I firmly believe that all of us administrators, educators, publishers, writers, and readers need in large measure literature that addresses more of what it means to be ethnic *and* American. And I think that in our daily communication we benefit from reading the works of multicultural literary artists from diverse backgrounds. When we do communicate, we know that in addition to our attitude so much depends on the right word. When the preacher preaches, when mean children call mean names, when the trickster tricks, the word worker carries a primary responsibility in helping shape more of who we are.

And so I planned to help fill a need for multicultural literature by bringing forth *A Gathering of Flowers,* an anthology that, I hope, illuminates the glory, the splendor, the achings and failings, the flights and heights of a few of our "twenty-second cousins."

I have gathered here ten original stories, and one recently published, by multiethnic authors whose writing I admire tremendously. In fact, I get such a special feeling of warmth and excitement from reading the works of these authors that I think of their fiction as being bright bouquets. And so the title *A Gathering of Flowers,* which is the original Greek definition of the word "anthology," seems right in more ways than one.

In every instance, what I searched for among the

stories I gathered was, first and foremost, excellence in the quality of writing and the ability of the story to wake up the imagination, to provoke intelligent thought and to inspire compassionate answers for today and tomorrow.

The result is a collection of colorful stories of compassion like Kevin Kyung's "Autumn Rose." Kisses and wishes tumble out of Gary Soto's "First Love." Humor tickles us in the offering "Upstream" by Gerald Haslam. Mysticism and hope highlight the Al Young tale "Going for the Moon." Intolerance troubles us in Jeanne Wakatsuki Houston's "After the War."

These stories find their settings in such diverse American places as the rural Oklahoma of my own "Young Reverend Zelma Lee Moses," the East Coast neighborhood of Lois Lowry's "The Harringtons' Daughter," the urban San Francisco Tenderloin district of Maxine Hong Kingston's "Twisters and Shouters," and the Chicago Latino barrio of Ana Castillo's "Christmas Story of the Golden Cockroach."

What it has meant to be young in America across time, as well as across cultural boundaries and geographical settings, is a current here, too. Gerald Vizenor's "Almost a Whole Trickster," our first story about being young in America, reminds us that Native Americans were the first Americans. As we continue to read the tales written by Japanese Americans, white

Americans, African Americans and Latino Americans, we sometimes stroll awhile beside the picturesque roads leading to the small towns and big cities and rural settings where immigrants in a new world have cultivated the colored and colorful gardens of their lives season after season. We finish our gathering of stories journeying to Rick Wernli's strange, fantastic "Colony" with its beginnings and roots in Omaha. This story envisions for us what it is we would miss if there ever should cease to be an America.

While you read this gathering of stories, we hope you find a fable here, a fantasy there, an extraordinary focus, and surprising turns of plots, patterns and rhythms. May you enjoy again and again the beauty of the word when and wherever it flourishes here, and may you come away with a feeling for the special promise of what it is to be young in America.

Joyce Carol Thomas

A GATHERING
OF FLOWERS

ALMOST A
WHOLE TRICKSTER

Gerald Vizenor

Uncle Clement told me last night that he knows *almost* everything. Almost, that's his nickname and favorite word in stories, lives with me and my mother in a narrow house on the Leech Lake Chippewa Indian Reservation in northern Minnesota.

Last night, just before dark, we drove into town to meet my cousin at the bus depot and to buy rainbow ice cream in thick brown cones. Almost sat in the backseat of our old car and started his stories the minute we were on the dirt road around the north side of the lake to town. The wheels bounced and the car doors shuddered and raised thick clouds of dust. He told me about the time he almost started an ice cream store when he came back from the army. My mother laughed and turned to the side. The car rattled on the washboard road. She shouted, "I heard that one before!"

"Almost!" he shouted back.

"What almost happened?" I asked. My voice bounced with the car.

"Well, it was winter then," he said. Fine brown dust settled on his head and the shoulders of his overcoat. "Too cold for ice cream in the woods, but the idea came to mind in the summer, almost."

"Almost, you know almost everything about nothing," my mother shouted and then laughed, "or almost nothing about almost everything."

"Pincher, we're almost to the ice cream," he said, and brushed me on the head with his hard right hand. He did that to ignore what my mother said about what he knows. Clouds of dust covered the trees behind us on both sides of the road.

Almost is my great-uncle and he decides on our nicknames, even the nicknames for my cousins who live in the cities and visit the reservation in the summer. Pincher, the name he gave me, was natural because I pinched my way through childhood. I learned about the world between two fingers. I pinched everything, or *almost* everything as my uncle would say. I pinched animals, insects, leaves, water, fish, ice cream, the moist night air, winter breath, snow, and even words, the words I could see, or almost see. I pinched the words and learned how to speak sooner than my cousins. Pinched words are easier to remember. Some words, like *government* and *grammar,* are unnatural, never seen and never pinched. Who could pinch a word like grammar?

Almost named me last winter when my grandmother was sick with pneumonia and died on the way to the public health hospital. She had no teeth and covered her mouth when she smiled, almost a child. I sat in the backseat of the car and held her thin brown hand. Even her veins were hidden, it was so cold that night. On the road we pinched summer words over the hard snow and ice. She smiled and said *papakine, papakine,* over and over. That means cricket or grasshopper in our tribal language and we pinched that word together. We pinched *papakine* in the backseat of our cold car on the way to the hospital. Later she whispered *bisanagami sibi,* the river is still, and then she died. My mother straightened my grandmother's fingers, but later, at the wake in our house, she'd pinched a summer word and we could see that. She was buried in the cold earth with a warm word between her fingers. That's when my uncle gave me my nickname.

Almost never told lies, but he used the word *almost* to stretch the truth like a tribal trickster, my mother told me. The trickster is a character in stories, an animal, or person, even a tree at times, who pretends the world can be stopped with words, and he frees the world in stories. Almost said the trickster is almost a man and almost a woman, and almost a child, a clown, who laughs and plays games with words in stories. The trickster is almost a free spirit. Almost told me about the trickster many times, and I think

I almost understand his stories. He brushed my head with his hand and said, "The *almost* world is a better world, a sweeter dream than the world we are taught to understand in school."

"I understand, almost," I told my uncle.

"People are almost stories, and stories tell almost the whole truth," Almost told me last winter when he gave me my nickname. "Pincher is your nickname and names are stories too, *gega*." The word *gega* means almost in the Anishinaabe or Chippewa language.

"Pincher *gega*," I said, and then tried to pinch a tribal word I could not yet see clear enough to hold between my fingers. I could almost see *gega*.

Almost, no matter the season, wore a long dark overcoat. He bounced when he walked, and the thick bottom of the overcoat hit the ground. The sleeves were too short but he never minded that because he could eat and deal cards with no problems. So there he was in line for a rainbow ice cream cone dressed for winter, or almost winter he would say. My mother wonders if he wears that overcoat for the attention.

"*Gega, gega*," an old woman called from the end of the line. "You spending some claims money on ice cream or a new coat?" No one ignored his overcoat.

"What's that?" answered Almost. He cupped his ear to listen because he knew the old woman wanted to move closer, ahead in the line. The claims money she mentioned is a measure of everything in the reservation. The federal government promised to settle a treaty over land with tribal people. Almost and thousands of others had been waiting for more than a century to be paid for land that was taken from them. There were rumors at least once a week that federal checks were in the mail, final payment for the broken treaties. When white people talk about a rain dance, tribal people remember the claims dancers who promised a federal check in every mailbox.

"Claims money," she whispered in the front of the line.

"Almost got a check this week," Almost said and smiled.

"Almost is as good as nothing," she said back.

"Pincher gets a bicycle when the claims money comes."

"My husband died waiting for the claims settlement," my mother said. She looked at me and then turned toward the ice cream counter to order. I held back my excitement about a new bicycle because the claims money might never come; no one was ever sure. Almost believed in rumors and he waited for a check to appear one morning in his mailbox on the reservation. Finally, my mother scolded him for wasting his time on promises made by the government. "You grow old too fast on government promises," she said. "Anyway, the government has nothing to do with bicycles." He smiled at me and we ate our

rainbow ice cream cones at the bus depot. That was
a joke because the depot is nothing more than a park
bench in front of a restaurant. On the back of the
bench there was a sign that announced an ice sculpture
contest to be held in the town park on July Fourth.

"Ice cube sculpture?" asked my mother.

"No blocks big enough around here in summer,"
I said, thinking about the ice sold to tourists, cubes
and small blocks for camp coolers.

"Pig Foot, he cuts ice from the lake in winter and
stores it in a cave, buried in straw," my uncle whispered. He looked around, concerned that someone
might hear about the ice cave. "Secret *mikwam*, huge
blocks, enough for a great sculpture." The word *mikwam* means ice.

"Never mind," my mother said as she licked the
ice cream on her fingers. The rainbow turned pink
when it melted. The pink ran over her hand and under
her rings.

We were going to pick up my cousin, Black Ice,
from the bus station.

Black Ice was late but that never bothered her because she liked to ride in the back of buses at night.
She sat in the dark and pretended that she could see
the people who lived under the distant lights. She lived
in a dark apartment building in Saint Paul with her
mother and older brother and made the world come
alive with light more than from sound or taste. She

was on the reservation for more than a month last summer and we thought her nickname would be *light* or *candle* or something like that, even though she wore black clothes. Not so. Almost avoided one obvious name and chose another when she attended our grandmother's funeral. Black Ice had never been on the reservation in winter. She slipped and fell seven times on black ice near the church and so she got that as a nickname.

Black Ice was the last person to leave the bus. She held back, behind the darkened windows, as long as she could. Yes, she was shy, worried about being embarrassed in public. I might be that way too, if we lived in an apartment in the cities, but the only public on the reservation are the summer tourists. She was happier when we bought her a rainbow ice cream cone. She was in dressed in black, black everything, even black canvas shoes, no almost black. The latest television style in the cities. Little did my uncle know that her reservation nickname would describe a modern style of clothes. We sat in the backseat on the way back to our house. We could smell the dust in the dark, in the tunnel of light through the trees. The moon was new that night.

"Almost said he would buy me my first bicycle when he gets his claims money," I told Black Ice. She brushed her clothes, there was too much dust.

"I should've brought my new mountain bike," she

said. "I don't use it much though—too much traffic and you have to worry about it being stolen."

"Should we go canoeing? We have a canoe."

"Did you get television yet?" asked Black Ice.

"Yes," I boasted, "my mother won a big screen with a dish and everything at a bingo game on the reservation." We never watched much television though.

"Really?"

"Yes, we can get more than a hundred channels."

"On the reservation?"

"Yes, and bingo too."

"Well, here we are, paradise at the end of a dust cloud," my mother announced as she turned down the trail to our house on the lake. The headlights held the eyes of animals, a raccoon, and we could smell a skunk in the distance. Low branches brushed the side of the car and whipped through the open windows. The dogs barked and ran ahead of the car; we were home. We sat in the car for a few minutes and listened to the night. The dogs were panting. Mosquitoes, so big we called them the state bird, landed on our arms, bare knuckles, and warm shoulder blades. The water was calm and seemed to hold back a secret dark blue light from the bottom of the lake. One loon called and another answered. One thin wave rippled over the stones on the shore. We ducked mosquitoes and went into the house. We were tired, and too tired in the morning to appreciate the plan to carve a trickster from a block of ice.

Pig Foot lived alone on an island. He came down to the wooden dock to meet us in the morning. We were out on the lake before dawn, my uncle at the back of the canoe in his overcoat. We paddled and he steered us around the point of the island where bald eagles nested.

"Pig Foot?" questioned Black Ice.

"Almost gave him that nickname," I whispered to my cousin as we came closer to the dock. "Watch his little feet—he prances like a pig when he talks. The people in town swear his feet are hard and cloven."

"Are they?"

"No," I whispered as the canoe touched the dock.

"Almost," shouted Pig Foot.

"Almost," said Almost. "Pincher, you know him from the funeral, and this lady is from the city; we named her Black Ice."

"*Makate Mikwam,*" said Pig Foot. "Black ice comes with the white man and roads. No black ice on the island." He tied the canoe to the dock and patted his thighs with his open hands. The words *makate mikwam* mean black ice.

Black Ice looked down at Pig Foot's feet when she stepped out of the canoe. He wore black overshoes.

The toes were turned out. She watched him prance on the rough wooden dock when he talked about the weather and mosquitoes. The black flies and mosquitoes on the island, a special breed, were more vicious than anywhere else on the reservation. Pig Foot was pleased that no one camped on the island because of the black flies. Some people accused him of raising mean flies to keep the tourists away. "Not a bad idea, now that I think about it," said Pig Foot. He had a small bunch of black hair on his chin. He pulled the hair when he was nervous and revealed a row of short stained teeth. Black Ice turned toward the sunrise and held her laughter.

"We come to see the ice cave," said Almost. "We need a large block to win the ice sculpture contest in four days."

"What ice cave is that?" questioned Pig Foot.

"The almost secret one!" shouted Almost.

"That one, sure enough," said Pig Foot. He mocked my uncle and touched the lapel of his overcoat. "I was wondering about that contest—what does ice have to do with July Fourth?" He walked ahead as he talked and then every eight steps he would stop and turn to wait for us. But if you were too close you would bump into him when he stopped. Black Ice counted his steps and when we were near the entrance to the ice cave she imitated his prance, toes turned outward. She pranced seven steps and then waited for him to turn on the eighth.

Pig Foot stopped in silence on the shore, where the bank was higher and where several trees leaned over the water. There, in the vines and boulders we could feel the cool air. A cool breath on the shore.

Pig Foot told us we could never reveal the location of the ice cave, but he said we could tell stories about ice and the great spirit of winter in summer. He said this because most tribal stories should be told in winter, not in summer when evil spirits could be about to listen and do harm to words and names. We agreed to the conditions and followed him over the boulders into the wide, cold cave. We could hear our breath, even a heartbeat. Whispers were too loud in the cave.

"Almost the scent of winter on July Fourth," whispered Almost. "In winter we overturn the ice in shallow creeks to smell the rich blue earth, and then in summer we taste the winter in this ice cave, almost."

"Almost, you're a poet, sure enough, but that's straw, not the smell of winter," said Pig Foot. He was hunched over where the cave narrowed at the back. Beneath the mounds of straw were huge blocks of ice, lake ice, blue and silent in the cave. Was that thunder, or the crack of winter ice on the lake? "Just me, dropped a block over the side." In winter he sawed blocks of ice in the bay where it was the thickest and towed the blocks into the cave on an aluminum slide. Pig Foot used the ice to cool his cabin in summer, but Almost warned us that there were other reasons. Pig Foot believes that the world is becoming colder and colder, the ice thicker and thicker. Too much summer in the blood would weaken him, so he rests on a block of ice in the cave several hours a week to stay in condition for the coming of the ice age on the reservation.

"Black Ice, come over here," said Almost. "Stretch out on this block." My cousin brushed the straw from the ice and leaned back on the block. "Almost, almost, now try this one, no this one, almost."

"Almost what?" asked Black Ice.

"Almost a whole trickster," whispered Almost. Then he told us what he had in mind. A trickster, Almost wanted us to carve a tribal trickster to enter in the ice sculpture contest.

"What does a trickster look like?" I asked. "The trickster was a word I could not see, there was nothing to pinch. How could I know a trickster between my fingers?

"Almost like a person," he said, and brushed the straw from a block as large as me. "Almost in there, we have three days to find the trickster in the ice."

Early the next morning we paddled across the lake to the ice cave to begin our work on the ice trickster.

We were dressed for winter. I don't think my mother
believed us when we told her about the ice cave. "Almost," she said with a smile, "finally found the right
place to wear his overcoat in the summer."

Pig Foot was perched on a block of ice when we
arrived. We slid the block that held the trickster to
the center of the cave and set to work with an axe
and chisels. We rounded out a huge head, moved
down the shoulders, and on the second day we freed
the nose, ears, and hands of the trickster. I could see
him in the dark blue ice, the trickster was almost free.
I could almost pinch the word "trickster."

Almost directed us to carve the ice on the first and
second days, but on the third and final day he surprised us. We were in the cave, dressed in winter coats
and hats, ready to work when he told us to make the
final touches on our own, to liberate the face of the
trickster. That last morning he leaned back on a block
of ice with Pig Foot; we were in charge of who the
trickster would become in ice.

Black Ice wanted the trickster to look like a woman.
I wanted the ice sculpture to look like a man. The
trickster, we decided, would be both, one side a man
and the other side a woman. The true trickster, almost
a man and almost a woman.

It took us a few hours but in the end the ice trickster
had features that looked like our uncle, our grandmother, and other members of our families. The

trickster had small feet turned outward, he wore an overcoat, and she pinched her fingers on her female hand. He was ready for the contest—she was the ice trickster on the Fourth of July.

That same night we tied sheets around the ice trickster and towed her behind the canoe to the park on the other side of the lake. The ice floated and the trickster melted slower in the water. We rounded the south end of the island and headed to the park near the town, slow and measured like traders on a distant sea. The park lights reflected on the calm water. We tied the ice trickster to the end of the town dock and beached our canoe. We were very excited, but soon we were tired and slept on the grass in the park near the dock. The trickster was a liberator, she would win on Independence Day. Almost anyway.

"The trickster almost melted," shouted Almost the next morning. He stood on the end of the dock, a sad uncle in his overcoat, holding the rope and empty sheets. At first we thought he had tricked us, we thought the whole thing was a joke, from the beginning, so we laughed. We rolled around on the grass and laughed. Almost was not amused at first, he turned toward the lake to hide his face, but then he broke into wild laughter. He laughed so hard he almost lost his balance in that heavy overcoat. He almost fell into the lake.

"The ice trickster won the ice sculpture contest at last," said Black Ice.

"No, wait, she almost won. No ice trickster would melt that fast into the lake," he said, and ordered us to launch the canoe for a search. Overnight the trickster had slipped from the sheets and floated free from the dock, somewhere out in the lake. The ice trickster was free on July Fourth.

We paddled the canoe in circles and searched for hours and hours but we could not find the ice trickster. Later, my mother rented a motorboat and we searched in two circles.

Almost was worried about the time that the registration would close, so he abandoned the search and appealed to the people who organized the ice sculpture competition. They agreed to extend the time and they even invited other contestants to search for the ice trickster. The lake was crowded with motorboats.

"There she floats," a woman shouted from a fishing boat. The trickster was almost submerged, only a shoulder was above water. We paddled out and towed the trickster back to the dock. Then we hauled her up the bank to the park and a pedestal. We circled the pedestal and admired the ice trickster.

"Almost a trickster," said Almost. We looked over the other entries. There were more birds than animals, more heads than hips or hands, and the other ice sculptures were much smaller. Dwarfs next to the ice trickster. She had melted some overnight in the lake, but he was still head and shoulders above the other entries. The competition was about to close when we learned that there was a height restriction. Almost never read the rules. No entries over three feet and six inches in any direction. The other entries were much smaller, no one found large blocks of ice in town, so they were all within the restrictions. Our trickster was four feet tall, or at least she was that tall when we started out in the ice cave.

"No trickster that started out almost he or she can be too much of either," said Almost. We nodded in agreement but we were not certain what he meant.

"What now?" asked Black Ice.

"Get a saw," my mother ordered. "We can cut the trickster down a notch or two on the bottom." She held her hand about four inches from the base to see what a shorter trickster would look like.

"Almost short enough," said Almost. "He melted some, she needs to lose four more inches by my calculations. We should have left her in the lake for another hour."

Pig Foot turned the trickster on his side, but when we measured four inches from the bottom he protested. "Not the feet, not my feet, those are my feet on the trickster."

"Not my ear either."

"Not the hands," I pleaded.

"The shins," shouted Black Ice. No one had claimed the shins on the ice trickster so we measured and sawed four inches from his shins and then carved the knees to fit the little pig feet.

"Almost whole," announced Almost.

"What's a trickster?" asked the three judges who hurried down the line of pedestals before the ice sculptures melted beyond recognition.

"Almost a person," said Black Ice.

"What person?"

"My grandmother," I told the judges. "See how she pinched her fingers, she was a trickster, she pinched a cricket there." Pig Foot was nervous; he pranced around the pedestal.

The judges prowled back and forth, whispered here and there between two pedestals, and then they decided that there would be two winners because they could not decide on one. "The winners are the Boy and His Dog, and that ice trickster, Almost a Person," the judges announced.

The ice trickster won a bicycle, a large camp cooler, a dictionary, and twelve double rainbow cones. The other ice cave sculptors gave me the bicycle because I had never owned one before, and because the claims payment might be a bad promise. We divided the cones as best we could between five people, Almost, Pig Foot, Black Ice, me, and my mother.

Later, we packed what remained of the ice trickster, including the shin part, and took him back to the ice cave, where she lasted for more than a year. She stood in the back of the cave without straw and melted down to the last drop of a trickster. She was almost a whole trickster, almost.

THE HARRINGTONS' DAUGHTER

Lois Lowry

They said the young woman next door was mad. The Harringtons' daughter—they called her that, as if she had no name of her own—was mad. They meant crazy.

That was all they said: that she was quite, quite mad, and I was to pay no attention. The shades on the south side of my grandparents' house, the side that faced the Harringtons, were drawn during the day, so that the vast living room was dim. Grandmother said the shades were to be kept drawn so that the summer sunlight, glaring in this rainless August, wouldn't fade the oriental rugs. But I knew better. The rugs had been faded all my life, and probably for a hundred years before that. They were the kind of rugs whose reds and blues were supposed to be muted by time and the tread of generations.

The reason the shades were drawn was so that we would not be forced to glimpse the Harringtons' daughter, who was quite, quite mad.

"What happened to her?" I asked Grandmother.

By her quick frown, I knew I shouldn't have asked. "She had an unfortunate experience, and completely lost her mind," Grandmother murmured. She adjusted her glasses and took up her knitting from the basket beside her chair. "Frederick, may we have some music?"

Grandfather turned to the radio and played with the dial until the sound of a solo violin throbbed into the room.

"Brahms," he said with satisfaction, and picked up the evening newspaper.

I stared into the room, wondering what Grandmother had meant by "an unfortunate experience." Only this evening the maid, serving dinner, had spilled some gravy on the linen tablecloth. That was an unfortunate experience, judging by Grandmother's sharp look and the maid's intake of breath.

My train had been late in arriving the day before: another unfortunate experience, no doubt, causing Grandmother to wait an extra twenty minutes at the sweltering, litter-strewn station.

My mother, their only daughter, was very ill. One more unfortunate experience, and why I was here unexpectedly. It had happened so quickly: a routine doctor's appointment; some tests; some bad news; surgery. "Don't worry," Mother had said. "I'll be home in a week." But something had not gone well.

There were specialists now, and consultants; it had turned into two weeks, and then three. No visitors allowed, only my father. And he had sent me away, to this silent house where the shades were drawn and a madwoman lived next door.

I leafed through a magazine, with a glum look. I had overheard my grandparents describe me to each other: "sullen," they said, with distaste. And I suppose it was true. I was seventeen and had not intended that my summer would be like this. I had intended that the summer between my high school graduation and my entrance into college would be one of friends and merriment, parties and pranks: the kind of summer my classmates were having back home, without me.

It occurred to me suddenly that I, too, was quite, quite mad. Angry.

"Excuse me," I said to my grandparents, probably sullenly, and left the room.

The kitchen through which I walked was spotless and empty, not at all like other people's kitchens, like my own family's kitchen back home, where a bowl of apples was always on the table, where checkered dishtowels dangled from the oven doorhandle, and hastily scribbled notes and reminders were magnetically attached to the refrigerator by tiny metallic ladybugs and bananas.

My grandparents' kitchen was unblemished white, like an operating room. Now that the maid was finished for the evening, there was no visible food, no visible punctuation of color anywhere, only the dull black handles and gleaming metal blades of knives attached to a wall rack. The dull, churning hum of the dishwasher marred the silence.

I unlocked the screen door that led to the back lawn and went outside. Grandmother's carefully tended flower gardens still bloomed, though they had suffered in the drought; tall, pink hollyhocks stood crowded against the wall of the house, beside rigidly staked white glads, and at their feet, masses of pale dahlias drooped, needing rain. The usually immaculate grass was brown in spots. There was a ban on watering, Grandmother had explained this morning, her voice taut with controlled dismay. "The astilbe has died," she had said, pointing to dry brown fronds of what had been flowers in the shaded corner by the porch.

Now, in the twilight, all color was flattened to gray. There was no breeze.

"Hello."

The voice startled me, and I turned to the fence, mounded with honeysuckle vines, to see the Harringtons' daughter looking at me.

I had never seen her before, though I had met her

parents, previous summers. They were older than mine, with no children left at home. But their daughter—the madwoman who was staring at me now, above the honeysuckle—was quite young. Twenty-five, perhaps? It was hard to tell. Her hair was in a long braid and she was dressed in a cotton robe, loose around her. She was thin and tall, not pretty, but attractive, with big dark eyes.

"Hello," I replied, and went to the fence so that we faced each other.

"What's your name?" she asked. Her voice was little more than a whisper.

"Nina. I'm visiting my grandparents. What's your name?"

She laughed, a low breathy chuckle. "Secret," she said.

Did she mean that Secret was, actually, her name? Or that her name was a secret? I didn't feel that I could ask.

"It's hot, isn't it?" I said instead.

"Is it?" She looked around, as if I had called her attention to something that she had missed. "I don't feel."

Then she turned away. I saw, suddenly, that her hands were filled with flowers. The Harringtons' yard was not manicured, like Grandmother's, not carefully tended; but there were flowers there, thick and tangled with weeds. While I watched, she went to a clump of asters and wrenched some blossoms loose.

"It might have been here," I heard her say. "This might have been the place."

A door opened, and a rectangle of golden light appeared on the Harringtons' darkening lawn. I saw Mrs. Harrington appear in the doorway, peering into the yard, and I heard her call to her daughter.

"Come in now. We didn't know where you were. You mustn't run off like that. Daddy was worried."

It was as if she spoke to a child. Like a child, the young woman went obediently up the steps to her mother. "I had to get flowers," I heard her say. "I need flowers, still. I can't find—"

"No more, now," her mother told her before she closed the door behind them. "No more flowers."

I went back into the house, where Brahms still played, my grandmother still knit, and my grandfather had finished his paper and turned to a book. Later, my father called, as he did each night, to say there was no change.

My grandmother introduced me, dutifully, to people my age: great-nieces of friends, the son of the Episcopal minister. I spent an interminable evening with a girl who talked endlessly of horse shows, and went to the movies one night with the minister's son, who was younger than I and idiotically proud of having been expelled from prep school.

I played the piano in my grandparents' high-ceilinged music room. I read. I wrote letters. I took walks.

One night, late, as I was preparing for bed, there were screams from the house next door. I stood, stricken, my hands frozen where they had been buttoning my nightgown, and listened through the open, curtained window. They were not screams of terror, but of grief: terrible, anguished cries that rose again and again, finally subsiding in sobs.

No one mentioned it at breakfast. Yet surely my grandparents had heard.

Finally I said, "The Harringtons' daughter was screaming last night; did you hear her?"

Grandmother shifted uncomfortably in her chair while she stirred her tea. She nodded. I thought, for a moment, that she would speak of the weather: of the relentless heat, of the lack of rain, of the disastrous effect on her dahlias.

"Her parents called to apologize early this morning," she said.

"They *what*?" I asked, shocked. "*Apologized*? Did I hear you correctly?"

"It's very embarrassing for them," Grandmother replied.

"Tragic," she added, finally.

"What happened to her?" I asked. The question, though I asked in a normal voice, seemed loud in the silent dining room, against the thin clink of silver spoons.

"She lost her child."

For a moment I pictured a small child misplaced, somehow, its mother searching the house and yard, calling its name. But I knew, of course, it was not what Grandmother had meant.

Grandfather folded his newspaper and set it aside. "It was a terrible accident," he said. "On a boat." He stood, preparing to leave for his office. His briefcase waited on the mahogany table in the hall.

"I'm not sure I'm following this," I said loudly. "The woman's child died, and her parents are *embarrassed*? Is that what you're saying?"

Grandfather looked at me. "Embarrassed was the wrong word," he said slowly. "They are helpless. You'll understand that better when you're older."

He went to the dining room doorway and then turned back. "The paper says there is a chance of rain soon," he said, before he left the room.

That evening, thunder rumbled in the distance and the air was oppressively still. I wandered again into the dark yard and saw that the woman I had come to think of as Secret was standing alone, on the other side of the fence. Her hands were empty.

Almost without thinking, I went to Grandmother's garden and began to pull the few remaining blossoms from the plants there. The wilting pink hollyhocks, the limp glads, the dahlias with browning buds that would never open: all of them I gathered in my arms. Then I opened the gate at the end of the fence and took the flowers to her.

"These are for you," I told her. "I wish there was something more I could give you."

She remembered my name. "You're Nina," she said. "Thank you, Nina."

I nodded.

"Do you have a baby?" she asked in her low whisper.

"No. I'm only seventeen."

"Someday you will." Her face had no expression.

"I hope so."

"Mine is named John. He'll be two soon."

I didn't say anything. She stroked the flowers that she held, and touched them to her face.

She turned away from me, and I thought she was going back to the house. But she stood still, and began to talk in a low voice. "He's such a bright little boy, Johnny. But I didn't know he could unbuckle the strap." She looked back at me, and noticed the belt around the waist of my dress. "Just like yours, a little buckle just like that.

"Unbuckle it," she commanded me in a fierce whisper.

I obeyed her and undid my belt. It slid loose, and I held it in my hands. I looked at her.

She laughed oddly. "But you don't disappear," she said.

"Would you like me to take you inside?" I asked in confusion.

She moved away from me fearfully. "Oh, no," she said. "I can't go in. I can't go back. I have to keep looking." She glanced around her feet, at the withered grass. "But it all looks alike, the water. I think it was *there*—" and she dropped a spray of flowers to the ground. "But it looks the same here." And she dropped another, in another spot.

For a moment, she wandered around the yard, murmuring and dropping flowers. In my mind, for a moment, I saw what she was seeing: the relentless water that had closed in an instant over her child.

Then she looked back at me, suddenly. "Can you help me?" she asked.

"No," I whispered. "I'm sorry. I'm so sorry."

"Why are you here? I thought I was alone. I was sure I was all alone out here."

"I'm visiting my gra—" I began, and then stopped. I went to where she stood.

"I'm here because I'm losing someone, too," I told her. "And I know you can't help me, either. But I don't want to be all alone."

*   *   *

That night, when my father called my grandparents' house and said once more that there was no change, I told him I was coming home. It was raining, at last, when, disapproving, they took me to the train station the next day: not a downpour that would revitalize the earth and the ruined landscape, but a steady drizzle that cooled us, that softened the dry, set lines in my grandmother's face and was better than nothing at all.

My mother did not die, not then. And I did not go to college, not that September. Instead I stayed at home with my mother as she gradually grew stronger. Together we read aloud, and laughed, and she sat, watching, while I painted our kitchen bright blue. Then she hemmed by hand the new curtains I made from a fabric as vibrantly colored as rainbows.

The Harringtons' daughter killed herself. "Took her own life" is the way Grandmother put it in a letter, and she enclosed a newspaper clipping that used the same phrase. I don't know how, and I am just as glad not to know. Not knowing, I can imagine that she found a place that looked—that *felt*—like the place where all she had lost had gone, and that she slid into it, cool and welcome and unalone.

Her name was Sigrid Harrington. I had mistaken the sound for Secret. And as she had predicted, I did eventually have children of my own. In years to come,

I would encounter other secrets and would grow to understand the wish to draw the shades against them. Sometimes the memory of the Harringtons' daughter kept me from doing so. I wish I could thank her for that gift, the way she thanked me for my small and helpless offering of flowers.

GOING FOR
THE MOON

Al Young

The first time it happened, I figured, well, chalk it up to coincidence. We'd been talking so much in science class about the connection between how you think and what actually happens to you that I figured that maybe subconsciously, like Mr. Cleveland's always saying, I might've been hallucinating or projecting or something.

I mean, when I got home and Edrick told me somebody'd actually heaved a brick in the window of the bar downstairs, I went to laughing and coughing so hard he got scared and, for a skinny minute there, musta thought I might be needing some professional attention. I even put on my coat and went down to see for myself the hole the brick'd made.

Naturally, I didn't stand right in fronta the Ivory Coast where Nate and June, the dippy bartenders, could see me. I had sense enough to go across the street. I was impressed. Whoever did it'd done a clean, righteous job. Nate and June had boarded the window up temporarily so business could go on as usual, but

deep down I knew this was gonna put a hurting on
those suckers. Yet and still, something about it was
disturbing.

"Zee," said Edrick, "you don't seem all that happy
about this."

"When did it happen?" I asked.

"Before I got up. So it musta been in broad day-
light. I woke up to this big commotion down on the
street. The police came out and stood around, and
June was out there with her fat self, talking all loud
and bad. I thought it was great!"

"I'll have to think about it," I told my brother.

"What's there to think about?"

"Don't know," I said. "It just makes me feel kinda
creepy the way it all went down."

"But Zee, you yourself told me you'd been concentrating on shaking 'em up, didn't you? Or maybe
I've just been imagining and making all this stuff up
since you moved in?"

"No, it's true. I did sit and picture a lotta stuff,
including a brick smashing out their window. That
image came up a lot, I must admit."

"So now that it's popped out for real, Zee, how
come you're acting so weird?"

It took a full minute for me to think through that
one. I'm not into violence. At least I don't believe I
ever was.

Out of all the missed sleep and raw nerves the Ivory

Coast had caused us with that loud-ass jukebox of theirs, it was the bass that got to me. The damn thing pounded right under my bed like it was the Tell-Tale Heart or something. The minute my head hit the pillow, it was *boom-bip/boom-boom-bip!* I'm talking about every night of the week. And nights when I had some heavy studying to do for school or some paper or a short story to write, look like it got twice as loud.

Of course I'd call up and ask 'em to turn the music down. Usually, if it was Nate answering the phone, he'd just say something like: "Yeah, well, okay, it must be pretty rough on you, up there gotta go to school in the morning and here we are down here, rattling you all around in your bed. We'll see what we can do."

But June, she was mean, man! Cold! She'd say stuff like: "Listen, don't you think it's kinda weird, in the first place, to be living up over a bar? How come you don't move? This is a business we got going here."

"Now, wait a minute," I'd say. "What's that suppose to mean? Me and Edrick ain't running no business, so we don't count, right? Just so happens we like it here."

"Well, we do, too, and our customers got a right to be entertained."

That's the kinda changes the Ivory Coast'd been putting us through, only it was rougher on me than it was on Edrick because he worked between midnight and eight, the graveyard shift at Safeway. Why any supermarket thinks it's gotta be open twenty-four hours a day is still beyond me, but that's the way it was. Neither one of us wanted to have anything to do with the cops, so we never called 'em.

Also, the apartment, even though it was on the small side, was nice and got a lotta sun. Edrick had dragged home so many potted plants from the Safeway until the window side of the dining room was starting to look like Golden Gate Park. Okay, I'm exaggerating a little, but you know what I mean. I'm not exaggerating, though, when I tell you the rent was right. In other words we put up with all that racket and hurt feelings and hassle with the Ivory Coast because we liked being where we were, out there on Geary near Golden Gate Park.

The flip side, you understand, was being able to come home from school and there Edrick would be, usually just getting up and showering and shaving. So even with my little part-time bookstore job, which Miz Perlstein at Last Chance High had helped me get through Community Outreach Program, my brother and me still had time to hang out together.

I really like Edrick. After I got outta detention and Moms started leaning on that vodka again, the only solution was for me to go stay with him. I never knew our father. And as much as Moms and me fought and didn't get along, especially when she was juicing *and* smoking that stuff, I still missed her something terrible. Sometime in the middle of the afternoon, while I'd be working at the bookstore or in the middle of some class, I'd remember how Moms'd spoken to me inside a dream I'd forgot I had the night before. I worried about her, and wondered how long she was gonna stay down in Texas, drying out. Even though Edrick wasn't but twenty-two, that was old enough for him to be my legal guardian.

When I told Mr. Cleveland before class about what'd gone down at the Ivory Coast, he said: "I wouldn't feel too bad about that brick through the window, Zephyr. Just because the thought rolled around in your head, that doesn't necessarily mean you endorse that sort of thing."

"But I thought about it a lot," I told him. "And the night before it happened, I sat there on the edge of the bed, waiting to hear the glass go to shattering."

I liked talking with Mr. Cleveland in his office. He asked me to call him Wayne, which I would only do every once in a while. It never felt right. I mean, the brother was straight out of the sixties, the way he talked and thought. Even that big afro he wore and the dashikis he'd come in wearing sometime woulda looked corny on anybody else. But with Mr. Cleveland, there was something okay about that. I liked him. Somehow he automatically made you wanna show some respect.

I mean, he wasn't tryna force you into no mold or pretend like he was your buddy, like some of the people at the juvenile authority do. He was just tryna get me to do more of my own thinking for a change. Mosta the time anyway. I must admit there were days when Mr. Cleveland didn't make much sense with all that positive stuff he liked to talk. I mean, all the depressing stuff happening all around me was enough to make anybody negative.

"So you know what that means?" Mr. Cleveland was saying. "It means you weren't the only one in the building who's been bothered by the noise level of that bar. The possibility of that brick going through that window has probably been hanging out there in space in the form of a thought for a long time. It's a thought form that's been waiting for somebody to pick it up and act on it, that's all."

"You think so?" I said.

"I'd be willing to bet anything that's what occurred."

And when I looked at Mr. Cleveland, at the way the late spring sunlight was angling in through the dirty window by his desk and falling on his face, that's when I understood how much he himself believed in what he was telling me. I could tell by his eyes how excited he was.

"So," I said, "all this you're telling us about thought waves isn't just another theory?"

"Absolutely not, Zephyr. Thoughts are as real as microwaves or TV waves or radio or radiation."

It wasn't hard to see that Mr. Cleveland knew I still wasn't quite ready to buy all of this, even though we'd been kicking it around—along with atoms and biology and the universe and other mind-blowing stuff—since I got into his general science class and made it into one of my hyphenates last winter when I first came to Last Chance. A hyphenated class is when you take a regular class—like science or accounting or history or whatever—only you can make it, say, a creative writing class, too. That's what I've done with Mr. Cleveland's class.

And that's what I liked about Last Chance High. It wasn't just another alternative education deal tryna help you save face; it's saving my butt. I'm learning how giving is more important than to all the time be taking and receiving.

"The mind is a sending and receiving mechanism," Mr. Cleveland went on. "You still have a problem with that, don't you?"

"Yeah."

"And what is it?"

"Well," I said, "if it really works that way, then how come we mostly go through negative experiences?"

You'd have to have your nose cut clean off to keep from smelling all through the room that strong peppermint tea Mr. Cleveland liked to sip on. "Is that how life feels to you?" he said. "Mostly negative?"

"Sure, that's the way the world is, don't you think?"

"I used to think that way," he said.

Mr. Cleveland always leaves his door cracked, maybe so the next person in line to see him could see he was already busy with somebody, so I caught a little glimpse of Marlessa Washington out there in the hall. It was just enough to make my belly go to tingling. She was sitting out there, listening to her Walkman, kinda flipping through our textbook.

"What you've got to understand," Mr. Cleveland was saying, "is that the subsconscious mind doesn't know how to take no for an answer."

"How do you mean?"

"Yes is the only answer it recognizes. It only knows how to carry out whatever instructions we give it. It's like we saw in class with seeds and what happens when you plant them in dark, fertile soil, then water and look after them. Up above ground, it might not look like much is happening. But down underneath, down below surface, there's plenty going on. Next thing you know—*bam!* Up comes the beginning of some flower or plant. It's like magic. That's what thinking is, Zephyr—magic. It's like a magic seed you plant in your subconscious, which is like soil. Then all you have to do is keep watering and fertilizing it. That's what we're doing all the time without realizing it."

"That's the part I don't get, Mr. Cleveland—I mean, Wayne."

He smiled and said, "All it means is this: A good deal of the time we're planting negative seeds of thought, negative suggestions in our subconscious without even realizing it."

"How do we do that?"

"We're unconscious of our thinking. We forget that thoughts are real, that thinking itself is real. It isn't a fantasy or something we imagine. Thought waves are real waves traveling out into the environment, the same as any other signals. They go out and get picked up on frequencies, or wavelengths. This room right now is full of voices and music and pictures passing clean through us, or maybe bouncing off us. All we have to do to pick them up is snap on a radio or television and tune it to the right frequency."

"Whoa!" I said. "That's more than I can handle!"

"No, it isn't, Zephyr. You've been waiting to hear all this for a long time now. I only happen to be the one you've okayed to put it to you straight and clear."

"I'll still have to think about it," I said.

Mr. Cleveland stood up with a big grin on his face and said, "And check out *how* you think about it."

"Well," I said, getting up from my chair, "right now I gotta go rock and roll with a test in Miss Santiago's current affairs class."

"Last Chance might be the last of the alternative high schools," Mr. Cleveland said, "but even here T.C.B. is still in style."

And even though the way he talked sounded funny and outta date sometime, Mr. Cleveland had that one right. I did have to take care of business in Santiago's class. Either that, or lose some units. Like everybody else who'd either been kicked out of or dropped out of some other high school, I liked Last Chance. And I wanted to get high school behind me and get on with it, whatever that meant.

The second time it happened, Marlessa was with me and I, for one, got pretty shook up again, even though we both tried to make out like what'd happened wasn't any big thing.

I'd finally got up the nerve to ask her out, so that Saturday night we were just crawling up to the toll booth on the Bay Bridge on the way back from a Run-DMC concert in Oakland. Marlessa was driving her mother's car, a raggedy old Rabbit. I handed her some quarters.

Marlessa squinched her face up and said, "No, Zephyr, I got enough for the toll."

"But if you're gonna drive," I said, "the least I can do is pay for this."

"But you've already paid for the concert tickets and our refreshments."

"So?"

"So that's enough. Besides, at the rate we're moving, I figure it's costing us about a penny a minute on this bridge to get to San Francisco. And with my luck, there won't be no parking place around our building after we get there."

"You still live at home?" I asked.

"Sure," said Marlessa. "If it wasn't for my mother and her friend baby-sitting for Little David, I don't know what I'd do. Don't you stay at home?"

"Nope. Well, not exactly."

She didn't say anything.

What I like most about Marlessa is she doesn't come right out and poke and pry around in your business. It's the same as when she looks at you. It's never direct or, I guess you could say, without your permission. She always looks like she's peeking at you through a slat in a venetian blind or out the corner of a curtain. I go for that. I suppose what I'm tryna say is that she's kinda shy, but she's also, you know, respectful.

After a while she said, "Little David, after I had him, both my parents said I was gonna have to support him my own self. That's why I dropped outta school for a year and a half. But then Mama got to where she loved Little David so, she said I needed to go back to school. I thought so, too. So that's how I wound up at Last Chance, where I could make my own schedule and really do courses that did *me* some good."

"You thought much yet about what you might wanna get into?"

"Yeah, I wanna either go to Contra Costa Community College or else to the University of San Francisco."

I was amazed. I mean, it sounded like Marlessa kinda had her act together. I still didn't have even the shakiest idea of what I wanted to do. I was starting to try to think about it, though.

"But how'd you get it narrowed down to those two?" I asked.

"They both have good restaurant management training programs," she said, "and that's what I wanna do."

"You mean, like, manage a Church's Chicken or a Burger King or a McDonald's?"

Marlessa laughed.

"No, Zephyr," she said. "You don't need no schooling to run a fast food joint. One day I'd like to open up a place of my own. Something with style, you know, where food from different kindsa cultures could come together."

"Like what?"

"Like, oh, we'd have a little soul food, but I'd be careful to pick which dishes we'd do because a lotta that Southern stuff'll kill you, you know. All that grease and high cholesterol. Then maybe some Guatemalan dishes and maybe some Samoan or Chinese food. You know, it'd be like a little tastebud sampling of San Francisco, all available in one place."

I said, "I can see you've been thinking about this."

"I dream a lot," Marlessa said. "I don't think it's anything wrong with that, do you?"

"Mr. Cleveland wouldn't think so."

Marlessa rolled up the window to shut out the booming rhythm and rap the car in the next lane was blasting us with. I looked over, sure it was gonna be a car fulla brothers and sisters, but it turned out to be a bunch of wild-looking Chinese kids. The girls had Technicolor streaks in their hair, and the dudes all had 'em an earring.

Marlessa laughed again. "On second thought," she turned to me and said, "change what I said to Vietnamese food."

I was tryna picture what such a restaurant would look like; how the tables would be spaced and how the menu would look. I even thought about what

Marlessa might have on the walls and how the waiters or the waitresses would dress, and what the kitchen would look like. But it wasn't easy to picture. All I knew about restaurants was from the summer I worked at a McDonald's on Market Street, so all I could imagine was funk and commotion.

"Zephyr," she asked me all of a sudden, "are you still on probation?"

"No," I said, a little surprised that Marlessa would come right out and ask anything that personal. I tried to joke to smooth over the wrinkled-up feeling I had.

"No," I went on. "You won't catch me stealing *nothing* else again."

"What'd they actually nail you for, Zephyr?"

"Oh, I had this scam. It was beautiful."

"Please don't feel you gotta tell me about it."

"Okay," I said, glad to hear Marlessa say that. "But we thought it was pretty slick. We'd go in these big stores, ask the clerk for empty boxes for moving, and wind up looting 'em blind before we came out."

"Were you doing it for money, or what?"

"No, for fun mostly. Sure, we'd sell some of the stuff on the street, but mainly it was what me and my buddies did. I used to . . . Oh, I used to cop a lotta liquor that way."

"Were you one of those teenage alcoholics, too?"

"No," I said, feeling sad again. "No, I was getting it for my mother."

For a long time Marlessa fell back into her silent thing, acting like she was concentrating on making her exit from the bridge.

"You seen much of your mom lately?" Marlessa asked.

"No, just a postcard sometime. She don't call me or my brother much. Nowhere near enough, even though we tell her it's okay for her to call collect. Sometimes it really gets to me."

"Well," said Marlessa, "I see far too much of my mother. So what we got here is a situation that needs balancing. You need to see more of yours and I need to see less of mine."

I didn't think what Marlessa said was funny, but I kinda faked a weak chuckle anyway just to let her know how much I appreciated her interest.

"Uh-uh!" she said. "Now, here's where the problem comes up."

"What problem?"

"The parking problem. If you don't get over here where I live before nine o'clock at night, ain't no way in the world these people are gonna leave you a parking space. Makes me sick!"

"Wait," I said. "Don't even think like that."

"Then what should I do, then?"

"Just picture that you're gonna get a parking place, just the right space for nobody else's car but yours. Tell you what, let's picture it together and see what happens."

"Aw, Zephyr, here you go again with all that Mr. Cleveland stuff."

"Here, let's just try it and see what happens, okay?"

While Marlessa headed up Hayes toward her place, right there across from Alamo Park, I went to picturing a big fat space right out in fronta her house almost. At first, I was scared to try to be too specific and was ready to settle for any kinda puny parking place at all. Then something inside me said no, that since it was only a mental excercise or game I was trying out, then, hell, I might as well up and go for the moon.

Before I knew it, Marlessa was driving right up to the house. I could feel all those let-down juices settling in my stomach. All that talking and picturing we'd been doing, and we might as well've been in some kinda oil painting. I mean, wasn't nothing moving!

Marlessa's jaws were starting to get tight as she circled the block. It looked to me like people were even parked bumper to bumper in red zones and by fire hydrants and in places where it was illegal for cars to be.

"What's going on?" she asked. "This is worse than usual."

"Maybe somebody's having a party," I said.

"I don't hear no music," she said, "do you?"

"Are you still picturing that perfect space?" I asked Marlessa as she rounded the block a third time.

"I'd be lying to you, Zephyr, if I said I was."

"Well, I still am," I said. "And I'm going for the big one."

"What you mean, the big one?"

"I mean right out there in fronta your house."

It was so nice to hear Marlessa laughing again until suddenly it didn't seem to matter whether we ever found another parking space or not.

"I'm gonna drive over a coupla blocks," she said.

"No, no! Marlessa, let's just give it one more try. Go around the block again."

It caused her to do a lotta sighing, but Marlessa finally chugged around the block and eased up toward her apartment house again.

"See," she said, "this is getting old pretty fast, Zephyr."

And just when she said that, a big old van parked right in fronta her place started signaling to pull out from the curb. And that's not all. At the same time, people had suddenly popped out onto the street from outta nowhere and standing at their car doors with the keys in their hands.

"I don't believe this!" Marlessa said. "This isn't something you and some of your slick buddies set up, is it?"

The trouble was, I didn't believe it either. I didn't

know what to say. All I did was grunt and shake my head the whole time Marlessa was parking the car.

Then we both got to giggling.

"Zephyr," she said, "that was something. We're gonna have to tell Mr. Cleveland about this. He likes all this strange synchronicity stuff."

"Yeah, but . . . I was so busy concentrating on this parking space . . . we forgot something."

"What?"

"How do *I* get home?"

Marlessa leaned across the seat and gave me a friendly little lipstick smack on the jaw.

"Well," she said, "I guess now we'd better get busy and start picturing some transportation for you, hunh?"

"What!"

"I'm only playing with you, Zephyr," she said. "Would you like to come up and meet Little David?"

"But, uh, it's kinda late. Won't your folks mind?"

"Folk."

"Hunh?"

"My father doesn't live with us anymore. And Mama rode up to Sacramento with my cousin to visit my grandmama."

"Your mother's gone?"

"Yeah, but that doesn't mean you can come up there and show out on me."

"Then who's minding your baby?"

"Zephyr," she said, "you ever hear tella baby-sitters? I'll drop you off when I drive the baby-sitter home."

And that's exactly what Marlessa did. She let me peep in at her little boy. He was a cute little joker, too. Looked mostly like Marlessa, but he musta favored his daddy some. I still can't get over her having a kid and still a kid herself.

But when we got upstairs and Mrs. Jackson pointed to the crib where the baby was sleeping, Marlessa went over, leaned down and kissed Little David. She kissed him in a way that was real different but sorta the same way she'd kissed on me back there in the car. Watching her do this, something clicked, and for a second, I flashed on how it used to be, a long time ago, when Dad and Moms were still together and they'd tuck me in bed for the night. That cozy feeling. You know. With a nice sleepiness pulled up around it all tight and snug like fresh-washed sheets and warm covers.

Marlessa drove Mrs. Jackson home, and I realized she only lived a few blocks from me. I sat in the back, holding the baby. He was all cute and blanketed down and everything, and it was an okay thing to do. But it still made me feel funny. I sure wasn't ready to be a father yet.

When Marlessa dropped me off, I said, "Let's do this again sometime."

"You tell me when."

"Is next Saturday too soon?"

"I'll tell you at school."

I said, "We have a telephone, you know."

She said, "Maybe the best thing would be to send you a telepathic message."

"We can try that, too," I said.

I honestly can't remember when the third time was. I mean, after that, I kinda lost count. Maybe a better way to put it would be to say I quit keeping track of my thoughts turning out to be for real. And I think that might be because my whole way of thinking is beginning to get changed around. Little by little, this idea about thoughts being magic isn't such a big, humongous thing anymore; it's just the way things are.

More and more I'm looking hard at what goes on inside my mind and how I feel about it. I'm starting to pick and choose my thoughts, the same as you'd pick a cassette to pop in the Walkman. I like being in charge of the kinda thoughts I play in my mind.

If Edrick and his sometime-girlfriend Rosie have a fight, and he starts sending out all those bummed-out feelings, well, that's Edrick. I mean, I can be sympathetic, but now I know I don't have to buy into his trip. Or if down at the bookstore I'm unpacking some newspaper like the *Enquirer* or the *Globe,* and the front-page story is about how everybody on earth, by the year 2055, is gonna to be dying from AIDS, I know I got a least two choices. I can either freeze on a headline such as that and stay hung up on it, or else I can stack that information up against other things we're learning about epidemics and disease.

Fifteen, twenty times a day somebody will be tryna sell me some crack, and I'll stop and think about what smoking it is gonna do to my mind, to this thought player of mine. I already know what weed and vodka used to do to Moms, and I see what dope is doing to other people I know, so I don't have to think too hard. Every few weeks, look like, somebody at Last Chance or one of my running buddies from the old neighborhood, over in Western Addition, would burn theirself out or catch some disease or just up and die all of a sudden.

I still felt like living for a long time, and I wish I could say there was a happy ending to this story, but I'm still living it out.

All I can report for sure right now—since mosta this is still so new to me—is that if the city keeps cutting back Last Chance's budget, pretty soon it won't exist no more. And this joint is too good a thing to lose. Mr. Cleveland keeps me up on all such as that.

"So what can we do about it?" I asked him.

"All you can do, Zephyr, is pass on anything good

you think you might've picked up here. You know that rhyme of mine—'Hold on to what's alive and forget the other jive.' "

The other day when I got home, the Ivory Coast was all boarded up. Not just the window; the whole place! There was a sign pasted on that very window the brick'd sailed through. The Board of Health was shutting 'em down. Probably for being too nasty, I guess.

As I stood out there on Geary in the rain and read it, every word on the notice was like an M&M melting on your tongue, or maybe even like sitting in the movies and chewing on a Jujyfruit. I swear, I didn't have a thing to do with that. Still, I couldn't wait till Edrick got home to see it.

It's no accident, though, that Marlessa's starting to test out some of these mind games, or whatever you wanna call 'em. Now, since so much interesting stuff has been happening to me, Edrick and his girlfriend Rosie are sort of testing it out. Last week Edrick told me Safeway was finally gonna move him out of that graveyard slot, where he's mainly been stocking shelves all night, and put him on the day shift as an apprentice checker.

When I asked Edrick how he felt about this, he said: "Well, I have been wanting a change for a long time. But I'm not sure I can make the switch all that easy. It's so peaceful there at night."

"Maybe," I said, just to get his goat, "this is the result of something Rosie's been concentrating on. She never was crazy about the hours you worked."

"Hmmm," said Edrick. "I don't know about all this brainwashing stuff."

"Let's just keep on sending Moms them good thoughts," I told him.

For the last couple of weeks, every night before I fall asleep, I been picturing Moms hard, imagining her getting well down there in Texas. I started doing this after I noticed how often somebody would either call me when I thought about 'em deep, or else I'd run into 'em. Some kinda way they'd show up. Me and Marlessa, we've been getting outrageous with it.

Guess what?

Moms called long distance from Houston this morning just when I was rushing out of the house to catch the bus to school.

"Hey, Moms," I said, all outta breath from dashing back up the steps, praying I could pick it up before that last ring.

"Hi, Zee," she said, all staticky. It wasn't the best connection in the world.

"What's going on? Is anything wrong?"

"No, are you and Edrick all right?"

"We're doing just fine. You get that last money order we sent?"

"Yeah, Zee, yeah, I got it. You're the best two boys a mother could wish for."

When she said that, I froze up a little. Moms never talked that way much, not that I can remember.

"Moms, you sound different."

"Different? How?"

"You sound better."

Even through all that long distance static and space, I could hear the little sniffling and funny breathing she was doing at the other end. So I wasn't a bit surprised when she came back on in this choked-up voice.

"Zee," she said.

"Yes, Moms."

"I'm sorry it's had to be like this. But I'll make it up to you two . . . somehow. I haven't had nothing to drink in so long, I've forgotten what it tastes like."

I didn't know what to say to this. Moms had told me and Edrick this so many times before, I wasn't sure how to react. But you know what? This time I didn't care.

"I'm into some new stuff, Moms."

"Like what?"

"Oh, just thinking more than I use to."

"Well, you never were what I'd call slow; just hard-headed like your father. Going by your letters, it sounds like you kinda like that school you're in. This teacher of yours, this Mr. Cleveland sounds like he's on the ball."

"It's the best thing ever happened to me, Moms. I'm writing a story about it."

"Yeah?"

"Well, never mind. When you coming home?"

"Zee?" she said, like all of a sudden the connection'd gotten so bad she couldn't hear me. "Zee? Baby, you still there?"

"Yeah, Moms, I'm right here."

"Oh, there you are. I can hear you now. Zee, there's something I have to tell you."

"What is it, Moms?"

"I love you."

"I love you, too, Moms. You coming home soon?"

She didn't say nothing for a long time. I stood there, looking down at the street where the #34 bus was just then creaking up.

"Pretty soon," she said finally. "I figured maybe right after school lets out might be the best time to come back up there and get resettled."

"Oh, that's good news."

"You and Edrick are gonna have to help me find a place to stay, though."

"Don't worry about that. You can stay here with us for a while if you have to. It'll be tight, but—"

"And Zee . . ."

"Yes, Moms."

"I even stopped smoking grass, too. But I haven't been able to cut out cigarettes yet. I'm gonna try, though."

"Don't worry about that, Moms. One thing at a time."

"I finally joined this outfit that helps drunks like me."

"Are you gonna let 'em help you, for a change?"

"Yes . . . yes, I am."

It took all the willpower I had to keep from blurting out all the stuff about thinking and thoughts Mr. Cleveland has been dropping on us. But something tells me Moms wasn't jiving this time. There was so much life in her voice, and I swear, this time I can almost feel deep down in my own gut how she wasn't as scared as she used to be. I knew there was a lotta thinking and concentrating to be done, but I was glad just the same.

"Moms," I cleared my throat and said, "me and Edrick can't wait."

CHRISTMAS STORY
OF THE
GOLDEN COCKROACH

Ana Castillo

We are on our way to see Paco and Rosa, who are getting ready to go home for the Christmas holidays, pack the four children, the assorted relatives who came to stay over the summer and never went back, the used clothes and appliances so treasured by those left behind in their Mexican village, load up the pickup-turned-camper with Paco's welding ingenuity, and head south on the three-day trip that leads to the tiny community in Mexico by the sea where Paco and Rosa grew up, fell in love and were married.

Their home in *Norte America,* the United States, is right in the middle of what now looks like the vestiges of a once-thriving area before the steel mills closed down and left the majority of its residents without means for a livelihood. Paco's extended family lives on the ground floor of the little brick house his father left him as legacy of the thirty-some-odd years he spent in Chicago working to support his family "back home." They don't use the storefront for much but to keep the junk Paco likes collecting and hanging on to for the time when he discovers what it will be good for. Right now there is a nativity scene in the window. Baby Jesus has not arrived yet. For twelve nights before Christmas the neighborhood children will come and sing Mary's pilgrimage songs. On Christmas Eve the statue of the Holy Infant will be carried in and placed on its bed of straw. The children love these evening meetings of prayer, song, and expectation, because afterward there are always special treats provided for them. Sometimes even a piñata, if a neighbor can afford it.

After the storefront area, you step right into a meager-sized kitchen with metal cabinets and a tiny table with a scratched laminated top, spotted black from a generation of service. To the left is a dark, claustrophobic room, floor covered with carpet scraps we gave them last year. That's Paco and Rosa's room. The crib for the latest baby is in there too.

Two steps up and you are confronted by two more rooms, equally dark and dismal. There are beds and mattresses scattered; none have blankets but are neatly made up with faded sheets. Since it's winter, I have a hope that the blankets are put away somewhere during the day the way beds are made sometimes where this family is from. I look around for a closet or bureau where such things must be kept but there isn't any.

There's an easy chair in the center of the room.

Paco is relaxing on it this Saturday afternoon, the children clustered around him. It is then that you notice it for the first time on an old library table when you turn around to see what they're watching. It has a twenty-five inch screen, or bigger if such a thing is made for the home, an ultramodern concave design with computerized mechanisms for color and volume control. It is so obviously in contrast to anything else in the entire room, entire apartment, entire neighborhood for that matter, that for a moment I just stand there watching Holmes beat Frazier in glorious living color before Rosa slips a lopsided chair with its guts spilled out under me and takes my baby from my arms.

It isn't long before the men have gone out to the garage where Serafín is going to build a wood-burning stove for Paco when he returns (in the middle of January!), when he will have to resume the modest body shop business he keeps his family going on until he finds a full-time job or when they just pack up and go home one day for good.

Rosa is fussing over baby. Her own children gather around, all cooing and staring with those huge, black eyes you see on paintings of little Mexican children—which is of course what they are, very perfect examples of them—Mexican children with tiny pouting mouths and full cheeks, just like my own baby.

Anyway, we have now moved away from watching the boxing match to the room where Rosa has placed baby on a small bed without a cover. This must be where her older sister sleeps. Cuca takes care of Rosa's children while Rosa goes out to doctors' appointments, conferences with teachers who want children to speak English at home too, offices that give coupons for milk if you qualify. Cuca is at the age where it is said she has been "left to dress the saints."

The children soon lose their interest in the new baby and are now playing trampoline on the twin-size mattress that's on the floor in the corner of the room. Did you apply for food stamps yet? Rosa asks. We can ask each other these questions because our husbands have both been out of work for a year, having met as prima donna welders at a nuclear power plant under construction that paid top dollar. A year of good wages did not make us all lose sight of our place in the spectrum of things or cause us to put on airs. Instead, we saved for such a time as this, and now even the savings won't get us through winter.

I tell her that Serafín went to the food stamp office but we were denied on the basis of having too much in assets. What did that mean? she wants to know. It means we have more than five hundred dollars invested in our three vehicles. But none of them run, Rosa says. I know, I say. The lady at the food stamp office suggested that Serafín junk them—then he could come back and discuss our eligibility for food stamps.

We talk about the children, their vaccinations, the cleft in baby's chin and who he may have inherited it from, and how Rosa would like not to come back in the dead of winter but Paco insists that the family stay together.

In the room shadows caused by the dim light fading through the windows and a shadeless lamp on the floor, I reflect on the children fighting over whose turn it is to make somersaults on the trampoline/mattress and recall a room much like this one. Me, the smallest, getting pushed on the floor as big brother and big sister bullied their way to jump on Ma's bed when she wasn't looking.

It's during this distracted moment during the lapse between topics when something, like the flicker of a candle's flame, catches the corner of my eye.

I've been aware of the belligerency of the roaches in Paco and Rosa's house and how they don't worry a bit over the possibility of disgusting company with such abounding presence but go on with their business of keeping the order of their infinite world as they have throughout history, since the beginning of time.

But what has caught my eye isn't a cockroach of the common strain; nor is this one of the lineage of winged grotesquesness that I've encountered when pulling the string to the light to the bathroom and am provoked to duck as if dodging bats. This isn't even the usual puny kind that makes its kingdom the kitchen cabinets, stove, bread box, and the shelves of the pantry.

This delicate example of verminous existence in modern civilization idling over the ripples of baby's blanket is shiny with a golden color no less brilliant than the wedding band I've worn since the day Serafín came home and presented it to me in a small velvet-covered box, on our first anniversary, just a week before my twenty-first birthday. That was during that ever-so-brief time of good fortune when he was at the power plant.

While I am inclined to brush it away and not smash it with the palm of my hand as I've felt compelled to do for a while in defense of my child's hygiene, but too stunned to do even that, Rosa's eyes began to follow mine until they, too, are on the golden cockroach.

"Paquito, bring me that jar," she tells the oldest of her brood, who stops his play immediately and runs off to the kitchen, returning in less than a second, or what might be half a mile traveled for the cockroach, which is by then determined to climb over the mountain that is my baby.

With the steadiness of a heart surgeon, using the tips of her fingernails, Rosa picks up the golden cockroach and closes down a lid with holes punched in it while the children and I have held our breath; she has done this without so much as bending one of the roach's antennae.

We are staring at the roach in the glass jar held up in Rosa's hand against the light of the shadeless lamp. The children's faces show ecstasy, and somehow I can tell no one but me is surprised that we are in the possession of what could be no less than a phenomenon.

"Give it some corn and for God's sake, don't drop that jar," she tells Paquito, who solemnly takes it from her hand and followed by the other children goes off to the kitchen.

"Rosa," I say.

"Yes?"

"That cockroach was gold colored."

"Not gold colored."

"Blond then."

"Not gold colored, nor blond. It *is* gold."

My expression must've become a complete blank because Rosa decides to honor me with a full explanation and assures me that she is also aware that golden cockroaches kept in jars and fed cobs of corn like minikings in some ancient, sacred ritual require an explanation.

"When Paco's father was a young man, already married with small children to support, but too poor and unskilled to do so, he went off to lose himself in the jungle where he spent an entire year." Rosa's story as told to her by her husband unfolds. "When he returned to his family he had with him a gold cockroach that he mated with a plain one in hopes of—"

"Reproducing golden cockroaches?" I interrupt.

Rosa shakes her head and corrects me. "In hopes of reproducing at least *one* gold cockroach. As it turned out, after much experimentation and tested patience, he discovered that one out of every twelve thousand eggs produces a cockroach of gold. Nevertheless, one time he had a pair of cockroaches. The life span of the cockroach is not very long, no matter how pampered it may have been. It took trial and error to find out what the most agreeable food for the cockroach was or at least its favorite, which is maize, as well as to be able to decipher the gender of a cockroach. Oh, my father-in-law had much to learn about the cockroach before he was able to have a gold male and female pair! He set out for the United States.

"Anyway, it was in this very house where he first found a room to rent. The store was occupied by the owner, who was an old Jewish pawnbroker. My father-in-law gave him one of his gold cockroaches, one of the twelve thousand offspring of the original pair no doubt, in payment for his room and board and soon found a job at the steel mill. The pawnbroker was very pleased with this kind of payment and always expected a gold cockroach on the first of each month from the young man who rented one of his rooms."

"What did the pawnbroker do with the cockroaches?" I ask.

"Melted them down. Although it required twelve thousand cockroach eggs to hatch before one gold one was produced, the landlord didn't mind that his property was being infested since it meant another gold one the following month. The house got so bad, the old pawnbroker's wife left him, as did the rest of the boarders. As much as he regretted it, he had to get out himself and join his family. He took quite a few gold cockroaches as payment for the house and left it to my father-in-law.

"He opened up another store, in another neighborhood, because soon every house on the street was infested with cockroaches, and since the gold ones are few and far between, and no one but he and my father-in-law knew they were actually gold and not gold-colored, no one else benefited from them. My father-in-law continued to do business with him over the years. Whenever he needed money, he took the old pawnbroker a gold cockroach.

"When the steel mill closed down, my father-in-law went back to his village to retire with his wife and enjoy the many grandchildren they now have.

He left the house to us since Paco also wanted to come here to work in the same trade."

"What do you do with the gold cockroaches?" I wondered out loud.

"This is only the third one we've found since we've been in this house. Do you suppose that the golden cockroach is becoming an extinct species? Anyway, the old pawnbroker still buys them from us."

"He's still alive?"

"Just barely," she sighed.

Serafín and Paco come in from the garage and Serafín gives me that look that husbands and wives give to one another when visiting that tells they are ready to leave and would prefer not to be protested. I wrap up the baby, slip on my coat, and we all make our way toward the kitchen, which we must pass through to get to the front entrance, which is at the junk-filled storefront.

In the kitchen the children are watching the cockroach-in-the-jar gorging on a half cob of corn. Rosa picks up the jar and shows it off to Paco, whose face lights up like a Chistmas tree. A look is exchanged between them and she turns to me abruptly and hands me the jar.

"Here. Take it to the old man. I'll tell you where you can find him."

"But . . . what about you, the children, the trip back home?"

At that moment, Paco sweeps the jar out of my hand. "I have an even better idea," he says enthusiastically. Opening one of the cabinets and reaching in, he pulls out a cockroach and, lifting up the lid on the jar, throws it in.

"What? You don't want the cockroach to be lonely or what?" Rosa asks, confused by her husband's actions.

"It is possible that this pair may produce another one of gold, is it not?"

Rosa nods, catching on to her husband's idea. "But how do you know you have a matrimonial pair?"

After a moment of reflection on the now two-cockroaches-in-a-jar feasting on maize, Paco reaches into the cabinet again, running a hand over the surface, and pulls out another specimen for the jar. "And just in case," he says with a broad smile, one of satisfaction that he is able to do something for the family of another man in need, he reaches into the cabinet a second time and casts yet one more potential mate for the gold cockroach.

I hand over the baby to Serafín and with the greatest care accept the jar of cockroaches from Paco, thanking them for their generosity and kindness as if I've just received one of those red sapphires that Imelda Marcos owns. Meanwhile, Serafín has no idea as to what's going on. I'll explain on the way home, I tell him, and I do.

* * *

The cockroaches have lived in the jar on the maize for three days and so far I haven't noticed anything that seems like the beginnings of multitudinous reproduction. Maybe they need more room, or maybe they need privacy, Serafín suggests, and takes it upon himself to test out his theory by transferring cockroaches-with-corn to a shoebox, which he ties shut with a string.

Days later, we have cockroaches as tiny as lint specks climbing out of the slits Serafín cut through the top of the box to give them air. It isn't long before the predictable happens. The entire flat is infested with cockroaches, and we have not only not spotted another gold cockroach but have lost sight of the original.

We have to find the gold one, Serafín tells me desperately, with magnifying glass in hand scrutinizing the backs of all sizes and dimensions of cockroaches that now parade over every flat surface, latitudinal and longitudinal, of our home.

It is a week before Christmas and the tenants in the rest of the building are outraged over the recent infestation. They are sending bomb threats to the realty office that manages the building for the landlord, whose name we do not even have the benefit of knowing. Serafín and I keep Paco's father's secret as well as the old pawnbroker has for over thirty years. What would our neighbors do to us if they knew we were the cause of this new misery?

So we keep our cool the morning that the masked exterminators appear at our door and begin spraying something that smells like the equivalent of napalm on the world of vermin.

The next night I am still sweeping piles and piles of stiff-legged dead roaches. Serafín has given up the search among the rubble in hopes of finding a gold one. But a dead gold roach is probably as good as a live gold roach to the pawnbroker, rationalizes Serafín, who had no trouble accepting Paco's wild gold cockroach legacy. This must have had something to do with his having been looking for work for an entire year, the new baby, and the onset of what is predicted to be one of the worst winters yet, all accompanied by his eternal optimism.

We are watching one of television's countless news programs late one night when a golden flicker moving across the floor catches our eyes and almost at once we have both pounced on it. It is Serafín who comes up the victor, marveling at the gold creature as it languidly treads over his hand, down his wrist, and over the plaid flannel shirt sleeve.

"Don't lose it!" I gasp.

"Don't worry! Don't worry! I've got it. Where's the jar?"

We get the gold cockroach in the jar with the perforated lid and without another word we know what we're going to do with it. This one goes directly to the pawnbroker.

"He retired in Florida," someone tells us when we find the shop closed down without so much as a sign to direct us as to our next move. With the pawnbroker gone, we're stuck without the slightest notion as to where to take our gold cockroach.

"We'll wait until Paco and Rosa get back. They might have an idea," Serafín says.

That's not until mid-January.

So be it, Serafín sighs. We hop the 22 bus, the jar in a brown paper bag under his arm, me holding the baby.

AUTUMN ROSE

Kevin Kyung

I never thought I'd fall in love. I mean *really* fall in love. You know, the kind of feeling you get inside, like your heart is expanding and turning to water or something. Like you can't live without that person.

I'm afraid if my father finds out about us, he'll break us up, forbid me ever to see Steve again. I'm my father's *Jang-mi,* his Rose. My father is a bit old-fashioned. An old-fashioned *Korean*. That's a world of significance, believe me. You see, it wouldn't be so bad if Steve wasn't white. A high school girl my age dating guys is bad enough, but dating a *white* boy— that's the worst thing I can do, like spitting at my father's reverend face.

Jenny, my sister—she thinks it's great. She's my accomplice. At nights, when my parents are asleep, she'll check to make sure their door is closed and signal me. My father is a very light sleeper, you see. And I'll creep downstairs, holding my breath, sneak open the front door and steal away into the night. Steve,

in his BMW, waits across the street, and we drive
away together.

We go to places, he and I. Sometimes we'll drive
down to San Jose or even Santa Cruz, or go up to
San Francisco. It's actually kind of crazy. Sure I get
paranoid, scared I might run into someone my parents
know. My parents go to bed around midnight, and
after I'd snuck out and jumped into Steve's car and
we'd gotten to our destination, it'd be almost time to
go back. So nowadays Steve and I just hang out at a
park or at his friend's place in Menlo Park, where
there's always a party.

We've slept together a lot. Steve's the first guy I've
ever slept with, and it's great. It's wonderful.

By the time he drops me off a block from my house,
it's near sunrise. I hurry in and try to get a few hours
of sleep before I have to get up again and follow my
parents to the shop.

We own a dry cleaner's in Palo Alto, near the Stanford campus. That's where I met him, in the shop
one day. A Thursday night I think it was.

I'd just gotten back from a late economics study
session class at the local library and was sitting behind
the counter, picking through my textbook. My sister
was on the phone with Joey, her latest fling, laughing
and giggling away. Father was off somewhere, and
Mom was at a church meeting.

I was frowning hatefully at the page on t-accounts

when I heard the familiar door chime and looked up. There he was, a bundle of creased-up clothes under his arm, walking in through the door. One thing struck me right away: his eyes. So much blue in those eyes.

"May I help you?" I said, putting on my business smile.

He smiled back and laid the bundle on the counter. "Hi. Yeah, when do you think these'll be ready?"

"You want them dry cleaned, right?"

Tugging at the strings of the red Stanford sweatshirt he was wearing, he said, "Yeah. Both of them."

Two dress shirts, one white, the other green, lay crumpled on the orange-hued counter.

"Tomorrow," I said.

He looked relieved. "Oh, great. Fantastic."

"Your name?"

"Steve," he said, and ran his fingers through his fair fluff of blond hair. He appeared dazed somehow, as though he'd just woken up.

"Last name?"

"Campbell. Steve Campbell C-A-M-P—"

"B-E-L-L," I finished for him. As I wrote up his order slip, I glanced up and he smiled.

He asked, "You go to Stanford, don't you? Think I saw you up on campus."

"No, I don't go to Yuppie-ville."

"Oh," he said, chuckling. He looked past me and

ran his gaze across the wall behind me, staring at the travel posters from Korean Air Lines my father had put up there.

"Your first year?" I said, holding out the receipt.

His look was blank for a second. "What?" His eyes, so blue.

"Are you a freshman?"

"No. I transferred from Cornell last year," he said, one corner of his lips rising in a half smile, as though he remembered something. "It was too cold up in New York." Taking the receipt he turned to go, then hesitated. "Don't I pay you now?"

"No, tomorrow. When you get your laundry back."

"All right. Thanks."

He walked out, and through the window I saw him cross the street and get in his BMW and drive away. Someone was in the passenger seat, whom I later learned was his girlfriend, Sara What's-her-name.

"He's cute." My sister had hung up the phone for the night and was standing beside me. "What's his name?" She picked up the copy of the receipt.

"Jenny, is that all you think about—boys?" I pinched her cheek, and she yelped.

Her smile was sly, wicked almost, the kind of smile guys seem to like. "Only cute boys," she said.

I didn't want to admit it, but I was already looking forward to his coming back. The yellow order slip

was on the open page of my book, and I looked at
the name again. Steve Campbell. Such an American
name.

It's not that I never had any interest in boys. I liked
them just fine, and though I wasn't sure at the time,
I must have had a puppy crush on Mr. Jenkinson, my
sixth grade teacher. He had this really cute butt. And
in high school several boys, all of them Asian, had
asked me out, but Father posed more than a minor
problem.

This Chinese guy—I can't remember his name—
used to write me all these love notes in eleventh grade.
They were pretty sweet. He was so painfully shy,
though. I might actually have taken some interest in
the guy if he wasn't so ugly. Pimples dotted his entire
face. When Mrs. McHenry snatched the love note
from him in geology class one day and read it aloud
for everyone, the entire room erupted in laughter. He
never wrote me another note after that.

Jenny, on the other hand, never had such problems.
Behind my father's back, she always found ways to
run around with guys. I've never seen her with a white
guy, though. Being a younger child, and my father's
favorite, she gets away with a lot. She's been seeing
Joey Han for two straight months now, a record for
her. I think she really likes the guy.

I suspect Father even knows about Joey. The Hans

are good friends of the family, and Father's always liked Joey. He's an honor student and on top of that plays basketball for his school team, the Lions. Popular guy. He says he wants to be a doctor someday. Sure, my father's impressed.

So anyway, this Joey, he comes in the shop one day—a rather brave thing, taking a chance on my father walking in—and leans over the counter and says to me, "I hear you're seeing this white guy. You guys really serious?"

He fluttered his eyebrows like he understood everything about our relationship, the whole deal. Jenny looped her arm around his, and kissed him on the cheek.

"It's none of your business, Joey," I told him. "You'd better get out of here before our father gets here."

"Look, let me tell you something, Rose." He glanced over his shoulder as though he expected my father to walk in any second; then, turning a serious face at me, he said, "Better watch out for these college guys. Especially"—he whispered—"these white dudes."

I was beginning to feel pretty irritated at that point. "Why?"

"The only thing these guys want is sex. They like Oriental girls, you know. It's really exotic for them."

"What?" I wanted to kill him. Right then and there.

My sister, exasperated but still smiling, punched his arm. "Hey, shut up, Joey. What a thing to say."

Whatever threats or knives or rocks I wanted to throw at him didn't make it over the counter because just then I saw Father through the windows, smoking his cigarette, rounding a corner. Joey quickly moved off from my sister and snatching up a copy of *Time* on the counter, began staring at a random page.

When my father walked in, he seemed pleasantly surprised to see Joey. "Oh, Sang-ho, what brings you here?" Sang-ho is Joey's Korean name.

Joey bowed his head in greeting, smiling up respectfully. "I came to clean some clothes."

He wound up staying for another hour, listening to another of my father's goodwill monologues about the importance of academics and life in general. Father gets off on these things; he loves nothing more than handing down his philosophical wisdom and learnings in life to the inexperienced, the young. Luckily, in his self-absorbed fervor, he never got around to asking about the clothes.

There is this one weird thing, though—the way I feel sometimes. I mean, I really like Steve, I'm in *love* with him, like I said before. But sometimes, like if we're walking down the street, I get real self-conscious. Sure it's kind of ridiculous, but I feel as though all the people are looking at us, at *me*. Steve's pretty affectionate in public, holding my hand when we go to places or even putting his arm around me. And I can't help looking all around me, the whole time, to see if I can spot another couple who are also out of sync in race—who aren't both white or Asian, etc.

Okay, so the truth is I get this idea sometimes that somehow I'm doing this wrong thing by going out with a white guy. Father, it figures, would definitely give a big YES vote on that one. What I mean, though, is doing wrong in the eyes of whites.

I look at it this way: If my Korean friends can look at a black-and-white couple and call them "salt and pepper" or something stupid like that—and they *do*—then I'm sure Steve and I can be, in people's eyes, something like "garlic powder and salt." I once told this to Jenny, who thought I was paranoid.

"Jesus, Sis, what's the big deal, anyway?" She was in the kitchen with me, cutting up potatoes and onions and other goodies for dinner, this spicy stew my father goes somersaulting over. "I mean, look," she said, waving her spoon in the air—an off-key rendition of what my mom does when she's in a rare combination mood of lecturing and cooking—"the guy's cute. He's in Stanford, obviously pretty intelligent, right? And he likes you, right? Even *Dad* would like him. So what's the problem?"

"If he was *Korean*." I leaned against a side of the

wall where the stove is, and noticed a new eye shadow, blue, on her face. "New makeup?"

She nodded, stirring the stew while fluttering her eyebrows, dangerously too close to Joey's habit. "Joey bought it for me," she said. She sort of cocked her face in a little angle and observed *my* face, like she's some appraiser or something. "You should scam on Steve to buy you stuff, too. What are boyfriends good for anyway?"

I was just about to tell her that some reassessment of her values was in order, but I heard the front door open and Father's familiar cough—from too much smoking. Father—he's always walking in at wrong times. Now, this was when he was being falsely, visibly, "aware" of his perverse smoking habit—*three* packs of Winstons a day—and to settle Mom down a little, he switched to Virginia Slims, lower nicotine or the like. These days, of course—starting promptly from the day I informed him they were women's cigarettes—he's switched to Marlboro Lights.

Anyway he comes into the kitchen, and Jenny and I switched our conversation to some made-up intellectual bull about the chemical formula of an onion. Jenny was taking chemistry that semester. With a cigarette burning and magically glued to his lips, Father said, "Don't you two ever speak Korean? What, can't you girls at least do that around the house?" He took a taste of the stew, looked blindly around, and when he found the pepper, dumped half the bottle in. "You girls give your mother an ulcer, you know that? She's afraid of you two forgetting your native tongue." He says all this in Korean, of course.

Now, Jenny's a character, sharp like a fox, Koreans call it. She squeezed our father's shoulder and, smiling her I'm-your-favorite-little-girl smile, said, *"Mi ahn hae, apa."* Sorry, Dad.

Father, grinning: *"Yau-woo."* Fox.

He left to turn on the TV in the living room, ESPN. It's always sports for him, that is when he's not watching some overly melodramatic soap/sitcom on the Korean program on Channel 26. Along with Mom, he'll—if you can believe it—actually *cry,* too, when a tearful turn of events happens in the lives of the stars, like the male lead who meets his father for the first time, coincidentally, fatefully, in the streets or something, since having been separated during the Korean War. Right. The old *Casablanca*-esque plot.

"So like I was saying, Sis, don't worry about it," Jenny said. "You know, a lot of your friends are jealous of you going out with old Steve, anyhow." She sprinkled more hot chili pepper into the broth. "He *is* cute." Jenny, always a big help.

Steve's a big help, too. I never really related my— okay, sure—*paranoia* to Steve, at least not in so many words. All he ever tells me is that I'm different from other girls he's dated. Aside from the obvious ethnic difference, he'll add—something, in fact, he tells me a little too often, which does not exactly take the load off my self-conscious paranoia. And since we're on the subject, last week I had dinner at Steve's parents' place. They live in San Jose, in this huge, gaudy house in a very tidy neighborhood, with your expected puppies—they *are* cute: Dodo and Bambi—and green lawn hosed and manicured to perfection. It was Steve's idea, having dinner with his whole family— meaning his parents and his sixteen-year-old sister. Of course I was pretty reluctant. I mean, we weren't getting *engaged*.

"They really want to meet you, Rose," he said, out of the blue, while we were in his room with a couple of his Stanford Yuppie buddies. He was even smoking this clove cigarette, and I thought I was going to pass out from all the smoke. "Mother wants to see who I go out with. You know how it is."

Actually, I didn't. My mother herself wouldn't want to meet my boyfriends—I'm not even supposed to *have* any—let alone make dinner for them. I wasn't, to be absolutely honest, too excited with the idea of being the tenth or eleventh girlfriend to grace his parents' home. I mean, I kind of felt trivialized.

"I'll feel awkward," I said.

"My parents are great. I told them a lot about you."

As it turned out, everything he related to them must

have drifted through one pair of deaf ears and out the other. They—with their stiff expressions and blue, inquisitioning eyes—had me in the court dock the entire dinner.

"You go to school with our boy?" Mr. Campbell inquired, for some reason having trouble looking into my face, as though I was this streetwalker his son picked up somewhere. *Our boy*—that almost made me choke on my steak.

"She goes to another school," Steve said, taking up the part of my lawyer, like we had this agreement that I couldn't speak in my own defense.

His mother kept sipping on her wine—went through about five glasses, in fact—and didn't bother to touch much of the steak, small as it already was, on her plate. She was, for some reason, infatuated with my heritage.

"Rose," she said, in her half-Eastern accent. "That's a lovely name. It doesn't sound very Oriental." Sip, sip, sip, "Is that Chinese?"

"She's Korean, Mom." Steve gave me a hesitant smile, which said: Aren't my folks a blast?

No, my love, and I'm about to experience indigestion.

"I fought in the Korean War," Mr. Campbell said, nodding gravely and striking a match to light his pipe.

We were quiet for a few minutes, with the exception

of Candice, Steve's sister, who was carefully snickering to herself and who kept looking over at me.

Then suddenly Mrs. Campbell said, "Oh, dear. Maybe I should have cooked some Oriental food. I have a cookbook—this Indian neighbor gave it to me—that shows you how to prepare Peking duck and, what do you call it, Mongolian beef."

"I think that's Chinese, Mom," said Candice, rolling her eyes, and just then she looked a lot like my own sister, Jenny.

By the time the dinner—a.k.a. nightmare from hell—was through, I had this overwhelming urge to jump on the dining table, do a rapid tap dance, and run very, very far from the evil house.

Believe me, I almost did, too. My paranoia, I think, grew from a balloon to the size of the Goodyear blimp. As Steve and I got into his car, I had to wonder seriously how their son ever made it into Stanford.

Now, I don't want to give off an impression that Steve and I don't get along. We get along just fine. *Alone,* that is. I mean, his friends are very civil to me—*civil* is the word. In their own way they let it be known that they're *his* friends. Anyway, we— Steve and I—do things, like going down to Santa Cruz Boardwalk and riding roller coasters, doing the romantic dinner deal, checking out the local movies.

We seldom get into arguments. Sure, he'll get a little bit uptight about some things, when we don't see eye to eye, but they're mostly minor, nothing much to speak of. I think one thing that does bother him is the fact that we have to sneak around my father's back, like refugees.

"Would he really mind, Rose?" he said to me once, in this serious tone, when we were in San Francisco by ourselves, in a restuarant. This was actually about two days after the disastrous dinner with his folks.

"You don't know him, Steve. He doesn't want me running around with boys."

He slurped on his Coke, gazed out the window at the weekend crowd bustling in the streets. Something was nagging at him, not just the sneaking around bit, but a bigger problem.

"It's because I'm white, right?" He frowned, lips tight.

"Oh, God, Steve, you knew that." That sounded harsh, so I added, "I mean, you understand. I really thought you understood that."

His sarcastic chuckle caught me by surprise, and it did him, too, I think. Steve wove his fingers together, elbows on the table, and said, "Understanding is one thing, accepting is something else." He is occasionally prone to little profound statements like that.

We sat still, wordless, until the waitress brought

our check, and when we got out in the mill of the crowd, it was way past eleven. He dropped me off near my house, said he'd call me the next day, and while I stood in the slight breeze—it is autumn—he peeled away into the night. A little dramatic, right?

He hasn't called me since that.

All right, I do love him. I really do. I called him twice and his roommate told me both times that he's not there. So okay, things aren't the best right now, you know? It's just trying times.

A few days ago I almost left my shift at the shop to try to find him up in his room on campus, but Jenny was very strongly against it. "He's got to call *you*, Sis. You don't want to look desperate." Her philosophy seems to me a bit extreme, and yet, having inherited the old Korean view of pride, I just wait.

Joey Han came into the shop yesterday, still wearing his uniform—big LIONS written in the front, "Han-Man" stitched across his back on top of number 69. His hair, solid black, was plastered to his head; he must have just come from practice, without taking a shower.

"Rose," he said, slapping his palm down on the counter, his face real serious, "listen to me. No, don't look at me like that. Listen to me."

"You're stinking up the store, Joey."

"Look, Rose, Jenny told me what happened." He took a deep, overexaggerated breath. "Forget him, Rose. I'm serious—"

"Just get out, okay, Joey?" For some reason I found myself, a surprise, breathing pretty hard, and I swear I wanted to throw something at him, anything, to stop him from saying whatever he was about to tell me.

"Damn it, listen. I know why he hasn't called you, okay? He's"—he lowered his voice—"with this new girl."

I kept quiet, staring at him.

"I saw them," he says, "together. I know his car, Rose. They were in the car. You don't wanna know what they were doing."

"Where did you see them, Joey, huh? There are millions of BMWs in Palo Alto, Joey. How do you know that was his car? Why do you want to break us up?"

I must have been pretty loud, because Father rushed out from the back, his face all frantic and worried. *"Mau-yah?"* What is it?

While Joey's bowing to my father, I run out of the store, toward my car. I ignore everything—Father shouting at me, the shop, the imminent traffic.

I didn't quite know where I'm headed until I get there, when I finally turn off the engine in a parking lot; students with backpacks stroll the campus—bicyclers, walkers, runners. Idiotically, half-heartedly, I search the lot for Steve's BMW as I walk toward the ancient-looking cathedral, where I used to meet him for lunch when we first started seeing each other, three months ago.

I sit on a bench and gaze all around me, knowing I won't see Steve there, bent over tying his shoelaces, slapping a friend's back, or just laughing. There are couples here and there—I even spot this Asian guy with a white girl, both wearing matching red Stanford sweatshirts, holding hands, oblivious to everyone else. My mind goes: What if the guy was going out with me, and the girl with Steve?

Then, sitting there, I feel really foolish, wonder what I'm up to. I wait until the mixed couple disappears into one of the pizza shops, and I go back to the car. I mean, I'm telling myself he's going to call me.

Father came into my room at night, something he rarely does, at least not anymore, not since I started high school. I pretended to be asleep, left my eyelids slightly open. And in the slant of the hall light cast across the open doorway, I made out his blurry form standing awkwardly still next to my bed, his cigarette burning between his lips. His hand slowly reached to smooth my hair, like he used to when I was a child. Before we bought the dry cleaner's, when he used to run a grocery store with a friend.

Back when he first began calling me *Jang-mi*. Rose. Actually, if I remember right, there was this Korean TV show called *Bom Jang-mi*. Autumn Rose. Maybe that's where I got my nickname. I don't really remember anymore.

Anyway he finally left the room, closing the door behind him. Opening the curtains, I looked out the window, down toward the streets. A week has gone by, but no sign of Steve. But any day now, I'll see the headlights to his BMW flashing from a distance, and Jenny will signal me, and I'll sneak down outside to meet Steve. And we'll drive away together.

YOUNG REVEREND
ZELMA LEE MOSES

Joyce Carol Thomas

A hoot owl feasted round eyes on the clapboard building dipped in April shadow at the edge of a line of magnolia and redbud trees.

The owl peered through the budding branches until he focused on the kitchen, in which a mother, brown and fluffy as buttermilk biscuits, stood by the muslin-draped window, opening glass jars of yams, okra, tomatoes, spinach, and cabbage and stirred the muted colors in a big, black cast-iron pot. Then she raised the fire until she set the harvest green and red colors of the vegetables bubbling before fitting the heavy lid in place and lowering the flame.

She watched the blaze, listening to the slow fire make the food sing in low lullaby.

When it was time, she ladled the stew onto warmed platters, sliced warm-smelling red-pepper corn bread into generous wedges, and poured golden tea into three fat clay mugs.

"Dinner!" her voice sang.

"Coming, Mama," said tall Zelma, who was leaning over stoking the fire in the wood fireplace. Her shadow echoed an angular face, backlit by the light from the flames.

When she turned around, her striking features showed misty black eyes in a face which by itself was a chiseled beauty mark. Indeed, she gave the phrase "colored woman" its original meaning. She was colored, with skin the sugar brown of maple syrup.

At the kitchen table she sat between her aging parents. Her father, his earthen face an older, darker, lined version of Zelma's, his hair thick as white cotton and just as soft and yielding to Zelma's touch, started the blessing.

"We thank thee for this bountiful meal. . . ."

"May it strengthen us in our comings and goings," Zelma continued.

"Lord, do look down and watch over us for the work that lies ahead," chanted the father and daughter together.

"And bless the hands of the cook who prepared this meal."

"Amen," said the mother.

They ate as the quiet light outside their window began to fall in whispers. Zelma told time by how long the fire in the fireplace at their backs danced. She counted the dusky minutes in how long it took to clear the table, to clean and place the dishes in their appointed places in the cabinet, to scrub the black cast-iron pot until it gleamed black as night.

Then it was the hushing hour, the clock of the trees and the sky and the flying crickets said, "Come, let us go into the house of the Lord." And they started out, hands holding hands, down the red clay dusty road together.

Before long they were joined by Mother Augusta, a pillar of the community and cornerstone of the church.

The eighty-year-old Mother Augusta, who like a seer was frequently visited by psychic dreams, enjoyed a reputation as the wrinkleless wonder because her face was so plump no lines could live there, causing folks to say, "She either a witch or she been touched by God." Today Mother Augusta kept up a goodly pace with her wooden cane. Augusta and her late husband had broken the record for the longest continuous years of service as board members to the church. She was a live oak living on down through the years and keeping up the tradition now that her husband was gone on.

Today as the family walked along, Mother Augusta smiled at Zelma, thinking it was just about wedding time for the young woman. The older Mother Augusta's head flooded with memories of Zelma and how she had always been special, but one memory stood out from the rest. One April memory many years back.

The Bible Band of preschoolers had come marching into the church that Easter looking so pretty, and all the children serious, strict-postured, the girls with black braids laced with ribbons like rainbows. A few with hot-iron curls.

Each of the ten children had stepped forward and given a biblical recitation, a spring poem, a short song. The church house nodded, a collection of heads in a show of approval as one child with pink ribbons sat down.

Another reciter in a little Easter-egg-yellow child's hat stood up and delivered an age-old poem. Finishing, she gave a sigh of relief, curtsied, and took her seat.

Then Zelma, pressed and curled, stepped forward, her maple hands twisting shyly at the sleeves of her lavender-blue and dotty-green organdy dress. In white cotton stockings and ebony patent leather shoes so shiny and carefully walked in no mud scuffed the mirror bright surface, her feet just wouldn't stay still. Zelma couldn't get settled; she nervously listed from one foot to the other.

She started her speech in an expressionless, sing-song tone. No color anywhere near it. It was a typical Bible Band young people's performance that the whole church endured, as yet another duty, as yet another means of showering encouragement upon the young.

Zelma recited:

"It's raining, it's raining;
The flowers are delighted;
The thirsty garden greens will grow,
The bubbling brooks will quickly flow;
It's raining, it's raining, a lovely rainy day."

Now instead of curtsying and sitting herself down, Zelma stared suddenly at the crucifix above the sanctuary door.

She stared so hard until every head followed her gaze that had settled on the melancholy light beaming on the crucifix.

Then in a different voice she started to speak.

"And Jesus got up on the cross and He couldn't get down."

Mother Augusta had moved forward in her seat as if to say, "Hear tell!"

And Zelma went on like that, giving her own interpretation of the crucifixion, passion making her voice vibrate.

An usher moved forward to stop her, but Mother Augusta waved the usher back.

"Well?" said Mother Augusta.

"If He could have got down, He would've," Zelma supposed.

Zelma talked about stubbing her toe, about how

much it hurt, and she reported the accident she had of once stepping on a rusty nail.

"If one nail could hurt so bad, how painful the Christ nails piercing Him in His side must have been," Zelma decided.

"And so I think He didn't get down, because you see," she added in a whisper, "something was holding Him there.

"It was something special."

"Yes?" called Mother Augusta just as a deacon moved to herd the child to her pew. Bishop Moses waved the deacon back.

"I know He wanted to get down. Why else would He have said, 'My Lord, my Lord, why hast Thou forsaken me?' "

"Amen," said the first usher.

"But you see," said Zelma, "something was holding my Lord there, something was nailing Him to that old rugged cross, and it wasn't just metal nails."

Now the entire church had gotten into the spirit with young Zelma.

"Wasn't just metal nails," sang the church in response.

"It was nails of compassion."

"Nails of compassion," repeated the church.

"He was nailed with nails of sorrow," Zelma preached.

"Nails of sorrow," the church rang out.

"Nailed for our iniquity," Zelma called.

"Nailed," the church responded.

"He was nailed, he was bruised for our transgression."

Then Zelma let go. "The nail, the nail that wouldn't let Him down, the nail that would give Him no peace, the nail that held Him there was the nail of love."

"Love," shouted the church.

"Jesus," Zelma said, in a lower muted voice, "Jesus got up on the cross and He couldn't get down, and because He couldn't get down, and because He couldn't get down, He saved a world in the name of a nail called Love!"

It was all told in rhythms.

As the church went ecstatic with delight, somebody handed Zelma her guitar.

Another child hit the tambourine.

And the music started talking to itself.

"She been called to preach," announced Mother Augusta.

Bishop Moses, scratching his getting-on-in-years head, was as thunderstruck as the other members of the congregation. He flitted from one to the other as they stood outside in the church yard to gossip and to appraise the service.

One of the elder deacons opened his mouth to object, starting to say something backward, something about the Bible saying fellowship meant fellows not women, but the eldest sister on the usher board proclaimed, "God stopped by here this morning!"

Who could argue with that?

This evening as Augusta walked along with Zelma's family skirting the honeysuckle-wrapped trees of the Sweet Earth woods, they eagerly approached that same church, now many years later. Two mockingbirds singing and chasing each other in the tulip trees just by the tamed path leading into the church house reminded Mother Augusta that it was almost Easter again.

Spring was lifting her voice through the throats of the brown thrashers and the wood thrushes and the wild calls coming from the woods.

And in the light colors of bird feathers, beauty spread her charm all over the land.

Inside the church a wine-red rug stitched with Cherokee roses led the way down the center aisle around a pot-bellied stove and continued up three steps. Behind the lectern sat three elevated chairs for Bishop Benjamin Moses, Zelma Lee Moses, and any dignitary who might come to visit. Then behind the three chairs perched seats for the choir members who filled them when the singers performed formally and on Sundays.

The church had been there so long that the original white paint on the pew armrests had been worn and polished by generations of the members' hands until in spots the pure unadulturated rosewood peeked through.

The Bishop opened the weeknight service by saying a prayer. All over the building the members stood, knelt, sat, waiting for the rapture.

Soon Testimony Service was over and the congregational singing had been going on for some time before they felt that special wonder when the meeting caught fire. First they felt nothing and then they all felt the spirit at one time.

The soul-thrilling meters, the changing rhythms, the syncopated tambourine beats trembled inside every heart until they were all of one accord.

Stripes of music gathered and fell across the people's minds like lights.

Melodies lifted them up to a higher place and never let them down.

The notes rang out from the same source: the female, powerhouse voice of Zelma Lee Moses. She bounced high on the balls of her feet as she picked the guitar's steely strings, moving them like silk ribbons. The congregation felt the notes tickling from midway in their spines and on down to the last nerve in their toes.

Zelma gave a sweet holler, then lowered her voice to sing so persuasively that the people's shoulders couldn't stay still, just had to move into the electrifying rhythm and get happy.

Zelma gospel-skipped so quick in her deep-blue robe whirling with every step she took, somebody had to unwrap the guitar from around her neck. She was a jubilee all by herself.

And the people sang out her name, her first two names, so musically that they couldn't call one without calling the other: *Zelma Lee*.

Perfect Peace Baptist Church of Sweet Earth, Oklahoma, sat smack-dab in the middle of a meadow near the piney woods. This zigzag board wooden building with the pot-bellied stove in its center served as Zelma Lee Moses's second home.

Here she sang so compellingly that shiny-feathered crows from high in the treetops winged lower, above the red clay earth, roosted on black tupelo tree branches, peeked in the church window and bobbed their heads, flapped their glossy feathers, cawing in time to the quickened-to-perfection, steady beat.

Reverend Zelma Lee Moses closed her eyes and reached for the impossible note made possible by practice and a gift from God. Row after row of worshippers commenced to moaning watching her soul, limited only by her earthly body, full and brimming over, hop off the pulpit. She sang, "Lord, just a little mercy's all I need."

And she didn't need a microphone.

"Look a yonder, just a skipping with the gift and the rhythm of God." Mother Augusta over in the Amen Corner clapped her hands in syncopated time. At home, Sister Moses, Zelma's blood mother, was the woman of the house, but in the sanctuary Mother Augusta, the mother of the church, was in charge.

Zelma began and ended every sermon with the number "Lord, Just a Little Mercy's All I Need."

The sound tambourined and the Sweet Earth sisters swooned and swooned, the ushers waved their prettiest embroidered handkerchiefs under the noses of the overcome, but they couldn't revive the fainting women as long as young Reverend Zelma Lee Moses dipped into her soul and crooned,

> *"Lord, just a little mercy's all I need.*
> *If I have sinned in any way,*
> *Down on my knees I'll stay and pray,*
> *Lord, just a little mercy's all I need."*

How her silver voice swooped over the words, coloring them a mystery color that did not exist except in the mind which received it, forgot it, then gave it back.

Daniel, a newcomer who'd only been in town for

one year, wanted Zelma to pay him some attention; how she had stayed unattached puzzled him. He knew the statuesque Reverend Zelma Lee Moses easily attracted men. On this third visit to church Daniel saw how men flocked like butterflies to Zelma's color-rich flower garden, to the sunbows in her throat every time she opened her mouth to preach or sing. Out flew the apricot hues of hollyhock. The gold of the goldenrod, the blue pearl of Jacob's ladder. Daniel got a little jealous watching Zelma study the fellows, her camera eyes pausing on one young man's skin that rivaled the brown feather colors of a red-tailed hawk. Her admiring gaze directed briefly at the young man made Daniel itch around the collar. He turned neon red inside watching her watching him.

But it was on Daniel that Zelma's camera stopped scanning and focused. She saw his skin flirting with light, his inky hair accepting the brilliance like a thirsty canvas accepts a crown of black beads dabbed by a painter's shimmering brush.

His eyes shone with such a joy-lit intensity of sparkling double black flecked with the silver crescents of the moon that looking into them made her want to die or live forever.

Now Zelma, already so touched with talent that limousined producers from New York came down and waved rock and roll contracts in front of her, wanted to ask Daniel his opinion of the intricate offers.

"What do you think about this here music contract," she asked him one night after service.

"Rock and roll? I don't know. Seems to me you
ought to keep singing gospel. But take your time,"
he advised after studying the papers.

"Time," she said thoughtfully, and when she
looked in Daniel's eyes, she knew he was just thinking
about what was best for her.

"Think I'll write gospel right next to rock and roll,"
she said.

"Makes sense to me," said Daniel.

"What you studying to be?" she asked.

"How do you know I'm studying anything?" he
teased.

"You're getting lots of books in the mail."

"Oh that! I'm studying to be an electrician or a
bishop like your daddy," he said, handing the music
recording agreement back to her.

"So that's why you're always carting the Bible and
those big mail-order books around!"

"That's the truth," he acknowledged with a grin.

"An electrical bishop."

"An electrician-bishop," said Daniel.

"Uh-hm," said Zelma Lee in her most musical-
speaking voice.

When she took her time about signing the contracts,
the producers resorted to recording her mellifluous
gospel voice to see if they could find someone else to

match it who wouldn't study too long over the words in their contracts. But they never could.

Nobody else had that red clay memory in her throat, fat gold floating in the colored notes.

So they returned to try again and again until the young singer, after understanding as best she could all the small print and inserting the part about gospel, took pen in hand and signed the document.

That night her voice rivered out melodies so clear that when the music company visitors from the outside world heard the rhythms rinsed in some heavenly rain, they either thought of art or something dangerous they could not name.

Since the producers were coming with music on their minds, they only thought of songs and never perceived the threat.

The producers seemed so out of place in that place that welcomed everybody, common and uncommon, that they sometimes giggled suddenly without warning and thought that instead of stained glass they saw singing crows dressed in polka dot hats looking in the windows.

When they packed up their recording gear and stood on the outside of the church by the side of the road where the wild irises opened their blue mouths, Mother Augusta, leaning on her cane, bent an ear to the limousine and commented, "Say, good sirs, that motor's running so soft on this long machine you can hear the flowers whisper. Umph, umph, umph!"

"What?"

The music merchants leaned back in their accordion cars and waved the chauffeur forward. They eased on down the road shaking their heads, couldn't figure out what she was talking about.

One said to the other, "Whispering flowers? Another one of those old Oklahoma fogeyisms."

"No doubt," agreed his partner, hugging the hard-earned contract to his breast.

Reverend Zelma Lee Moses only sang so the people could rejoice.

"A whole lot of people will rejoice when you sign this contract," the producer had said.

"Will?" said Zelma.

"Of course I'll be one of them." The record company man smiled as he extended the pen.

And more people did rejoice about a year after she'd signed the contract.

The echo of colors flew across the airwaves. The song "A Little More Mercy" made women listening to the radio as they pressed clothes still their irons in the middle of rough, dried collars, watching the steam weave through the melody.

Daniel, in his pine thick backyard chopping wood, his head awash in the sound, wondered at the miracle of vinyl, catching a voice like that and giving it back so faithfully, reached inside the open kitchen window and turned up the homemade radio he had assembled with his own hands. The sound flowed out to him even more distinctly. He raised the ax, chopping more rhythmically, clef signs scoring the wood.

More and more people rejoiced.

Both Zelma's mothers, Augusta and her natural mother, ended up with limousines, if they wanted them, turning the dials to their favorite gospel stations, which always played their favorite artist to the additional accompaniment of limousine tires dancing down the road.

Zelma only sang so the people could rejoice.

And therein lay the danger. Preachers who had that kind of gift had to be around folks who loved them, for the devil stayed busy trying to stick the old pitchfork in. Zelma kept herself too wrapped up with her gift to notice the devil's works; those around her had to be aware, wary, and protective.

She preached one Sunday 'til her voice rang hoarse with power and her guitar hit a note so high it rang heaven's doorbell. And all up and down the rows, women stood up, their tambourines trembling like rhinestones.

Palm Sunday, the Sunday when visiting congregations from as far away as New Orleans, Louisiana, arrived with their clothes speckled with the Texas dust they passed through to get to Sweet Earth, Oklahoma, and the new gospel recording star; the visiting Louisiana choir, hot from their journey, crowded the choir stands to overflowing and mopped sweat from their curious brows.

Palm Sunday in Sweet Earth at Perfect Peace Baptist Church, the deacons with trembling hands, babies sucking blisters on their thumbs, folks so lame they had to wheel themselves in in wheelchairs, eyeglassed teachers, and farmers with weed cuts persisting around their scrubbed nails, all stepped out, in shined shoes, pressed suits, spring dresses, and assorted hats, coming to hear the female preacher perform on Palm Sunday, and she didn't disappoint them; she preached until her robe stuck to her sculptured body, wringing wet. She preached until dear Daniel, in an evergreen shirt of cotton and linen, Daniel so handsome she could squeeze the proud muscles straining against his shirt sleeves, until Daniel who had been tarrying for a year on the altar, dropped his tambourine and fell out in the sanctuary overcome by the holy spirit.

A cloud of "Hallelujah's" flew up like joy birds from the congregation when Daniel got religion. Still the Sweet Earth saints in front of Zelma with their mouths stretched open on the last syllable of Hallelujah, had not *shouted*, had not danced in the spirit.

Only one mover shook loose in the whole flock of them. And that was dimpled Daniel, an earth angel dressed in light and leaf green and smelling of musky sweet spring herbs, stepping all up and down and inside the gospel beat, a human drum.

It was just about time for Zelma to wind up the sermon and finish with the song "Lord, Just a Little Mercy's All I Need."

And she felt as if she hadn't done her job at all if she couldn't get ten sisters and several deacons moved from their sanctified seats.

The visiting choir voices behind her had sunk and their volume diminished. She was used to more call and response and certainly much more shouting.

"Why's this church so cold?" she asked.

Stopped in the middle of her sermon and asked it.

What she could not see behind her were the visiting choir members being carried off the stage one by one. The entire soprano section of the New Orleans New Baptist Church Youth Choir had danced until they fainted, until only one or two straggly alto voices were left.

The Sweet Earth congregation gazed so amazed at the rapture and the different shouting styles of the Louisiana choir that they settled back and, instead of joining in the commotion, sat transfixed on their chairs like they were in a downtown theater watching a big city show on tour.

Nobody told Zelma she had preached so hard that she had set a record for the number of folks falling out in one sermon.

She wasn't aware of the record she'd just broken because she couldn't see the Louisiana choir behind her, she only saw dear Daniel in a golden trance, speaking in tongues, Daniel who made her feel like an angel every time she beheld his face.

When she pronounced Daniel "saved" and accepted him into the church, she made a silent promise, looking into Daniel's deep dark gaze, finding her passion in the curve of his molasses colored lips.

Before the week-long revival was over Daniel would be proud of her.

And then it came to her, not from God but from the soft place in the center of her soul-filled passion.

She would do what nobody else had done.

Come Sunday, the crowning day of the revival, young Reverend Zelma Lee Moses would fly.

"On Easter Sunday," she announced, talking to the Church but looking Daniel in the eyes, "on the last day of the revival, on the day Christ came forth from the tomb, Church, it's been given me to fly."

Their opened mouths opened even wider.

The New Orleans New Baptist Youth Choir, scheduled to be in concert in Louisiana on Easter Sunday, took a vote and sent back word that their Oklahoma stay would be extended and that the Sunday

School Choir would have to sing two extra numbers instead to make up for their absence.

Since the Reverend Zelma Lee Moses's voice had moved over them like a mighty wind, knocking them from their perches in the choir stand and rendering them senseless from the mighty impact of her spirit, they could not leave, even if they wanted to.

"Young Reverend Zelma Lee Moses's gonna fly come Sunday evening," the ecstatic choir director chanted over the Oklahoma-to-Louisiana telephone wires.

That very night, beneath her flower garden patched quilt, Mother Augusta dreamed. First she saw Zelma Lee inside the church, making the announcement about flying, then she saw a red-dressed she-devil down in her hell home listening to Zelma's promise to fly on Sunday. Slack-jawed, the devil looked up at the church and the people being moved like feathers and got jealous.

"Flying on Sunday? Zelma Lee's gonna fly!" The next day these two phrases lit up the telephone wires in Sweet Earth.

The funny thing about all of this, of course, was that passion was playing hide-and-seek.

Daniel wanted Zelma as much as Zelma wanted him, but she did not know this.

"I want this Zelma," Daniel whispered to himself in the still hours of the night when the lightning bugs flew like earth stars outside his window. It was then he spoke, forgetting his Sweet Earth enunciation, in the lyrical thick accent of the swamp place from which he came.

As experienced with women as Daniel was he had never seen anybody like Zelma, and so he studied her carefully; he slowly wondered how to approach her. He didn't want to make even one false move.

Just seeing her was sometimes enough to take his breath away. Zelma had already stolen his heart when he saw her sitting in the pulpit between the visiting evangelist and Bishop Moses that first Sunday he visited Perfect Peace.

Because the visiting evangelist preached, Zelma was not required to speak or sing. It was her presence alone that had attracted him. He didn't even know she could talk, let alone sing. Even quiet she was a sight.

Hearing her sing on his second Sunday visit brought him to his knees. Folks thought he had fallen down to pray.

Eventually he did kneel to pray all the subsequent Sundays, but his belly still quivered like Jell-O even now remembering what the woman did to his mind.

And Zelma had never had so much as one boyfriend before. Since she was a preacher's daughter, she was expected, when it came to passion, to wait 'til her appointed time. Music had been her passion; music had been enough.

Then came Daniel. When she looked at Daniel, her heart opened on a door to a God she had not known was even there.

Daniel she wanted to impress even though he was already smitten.

Anything she did beyond being who she already was was needless, was superfluous, but young Zelma didn't know this.

As Mother Augusta might have said, "Humph. The devil found work."

The first thing Zelma did wrong was she built a short platform out of the wrong wood and didn't ask the deacons of the church to help her out.

"Didn't ask nobody nothing," complained Deacon Jones, he was so mad his trembling bottom lip hung down almost to his knees. "Got to drive a nail in at the right angle or it won't hold!"

Second thing Zelma did wrong was she went downtown to some unsanctified, whiskey-drinking folks and had them sew some wings onto her robe; looking like vultures roosting, they sewed crooked, leaving tobacco smoke lingering in the cloth.

"You don't tell sinning people nothing sacred," Mother Augusta clucked in a chastising voice to whoever's ears were free to listen.

"Sinning people! They nature is such that they misunderstand the mysteries.

"If they see trumpets on your head, they refer to them as horns.

"Now and then you run across an exception, but half the time they don't know *what* they looking at," said Mother Augusta.

And too, the seasoned women in the church primped their mouths and got offended, because for as long as they could remember they had personally sewn the sacred robe with the smoke blue thread that had been blessed and sanctified in a secret ritual that nobody discussed, lest a raven run away with their tongue.

"Who knows what them drunk people put in them wings?"

Mother Augusta, the human *Jet* and *Ebony* combined, kept a running oral column going among the older people all the revival days approaching Easter Sunday.

In the meantime Mother Augusta wanted to have words with the young preacher, but the members of the New Orleans New Baptist Youth Choir kept Zelma so occupied the female preacher didn't even have time for her own Sweet Earth congregation.

Even her own father, the retired Bishop Benjamin Moses, couldn't get a word in edgewise. Between counseling the New Orleans young folk, Zelma studied the Bible in the day and slept in the church house at night after falling out exhausted from continuous prayer. In the wee hours of the morning she slipped home, where her mother had prepared steaming hot bathwater and laid out fresh clothes. She refused her mother's platters of peppergrass greens, stewed turkey wings and Sunday rice, including her favorite dewberry biscuits. She was fasting and only took water.

But the community fed the Louisiana visitors. The gray-haired, white-capped mothers of the church, mothers of the copper kettles and porcelain pans, kept their kitchens bustling with younger Sweet Earth women. They instructed these sisters of the skillet in the fine art of baking savory chicken-and-dressing and flaky-crusted peach cobblers.

"Put a little more sage in that corn bread.

"Make that dumpling plumper than that," Mother Augusta ordered, throwing out to the birds a pan of dough that didn't pass her inspection.

She personally turned over each peach, seeing with her farsighted eyes what stronger, younger eyes often missed.

The young Louisiana people stood around, underfoot, mesmerized by Zelma, but Mother Augusta saw what they couldn't see and what Zelma's mother's eyes wouldn't see.

She prayed, Mother Augusta did.

Zelma prayed, but her love for Daniel had her all puffed up and half-drunk with passion.

Come Easter Sunday she would fly, then after church she would offer Daniel her hand, and if he held it much longer than friendly, they would be companions.

Every night she preached and promised to fly on Sunday.

Every night the crowd got thicker.

By Sunday night the standing-room-only audience pushed and elbowed each other in competition with the cawing crows for a low, window-level place on the tupelo branches above the clay by the window.

Oh, the crowd and the crows!

The church house sagged, packed to the rafters. And Mother Augusta ordered the carpenter to check the floor planks because they might not be able to take the whipping she knew Zelma was going to give them once she got started stomping the floor and making the Bible holler.

"Tighten that board over yonder," she ordered.

Another sound that added to the clamor was the hum of more buses arriving from New Orleans. Some members back home in the Louisiana church were so intrigued by the choir's decision to remain in Sweet Earth that they boarded yet another bus and struck out for northeast Oklahoma to see what the excitement was all about, driving on through the sleepless night so they could reach Perfect Peace in time for Sunday service and the promised night of miracles.

The New Orleans contingency was so glad to have made it in time, they entered the church swaying down the aisle, fingers circling circles in the air, uncrossed feet whipping up the holy dance.

As the evening lengthened, something softened in the air. Maybe it was the effect of the full moon.

The Reverend Zelma Lee Moses preached about wings that Sunday night.

The soft shadows cast by the full moon looked like veils hanging over the sanctuary.

She took her text from Psalms.

"Read, Brother Daniel!"

Daniel opened his Bible and quoted, "Keep me as the apple of thy eye, hide me under the shadow of thy wings.

"And He shall cover thee with his feathers, and under his wings shalt thou trust: his truth shall be thy shield and buckler."

"Read!"

Daniel found the next Psalm and continued, "Be merciful unto me, O God, be merciful unto me: for my soul trusteth in thee: yea, in the shadow of thy wings will I make my refuge. . . ."

"Read!"

". . . Who layeth the beams of his chambers in the

waters; who maketh the clouds his chariot: who walk-
eth upon the wings of the wind."

Now the great flying moment the Sweet Earth people had been anticipating for a whole week arrived.
The spectacle that the New Orleans visitors awaited
was here at last.

As she approached the platform, the young Zelma
Lee Moses began to sing the closing number, "Lord,
just a little mercy's all I need."

One sister let out a long, low holler. Transfigured,
a ghost took over her throat, and it was like a special
spirit had flown in through the open church window;
like the miracle of the cross, Christ ascending into
heaven would be repeated in another way.

It was too crowded for the people to cut loose. They
swayed backward, swooned; and the crush of their
numbers held each member up.

Now Zelma Lee Moses approached the foot of the
launching platform, the platform built without con-
sulting the deacons.

She mounted it and spread the arms of her robe,
revealing the drunk-people-made wings.

And the congregation hushed.

Neither crowd nor crows flapped.

Young Zelma Lee Moses leaped!

But instead of being taken up by a mighty wind
into the rafters above the gaping crowd, she plopped,
sprawled, spread out on the oak floor at the feet of

the frowning deacons, under the scrutinizing gaze of
Mother Augusta, dragging her wings in the sawdust.

"The hem's crooked. And the thread's red wrong."
Mother Augusta pointed, almost choking.

"Caw!" sang a crow.

Zelma scrambled back up, sure that the Lord had
not forsaken her.

Maybe all she needed was a little speed to prime
her wings: Recalling the way kites had to be hoisted,
remembering her long adolescent legs running down
the weed fields fast and far enough before the kite
yielded to the wind and took off, she opened her hands
and spread her wings.

And with her long arms out as far as she could fling
them, she ran, up and down the aisles, her arms moving up and down, her hands making circles. Up and
down the aisles.

Up. Down.

Fast, faster.

Up. Down.

Fast. Faster.

She ran past her future sweetheart-to-be and Daniel
saw that she could not fly.

And she could not fly.

Finally her mother said, "Daughter?"

And the people got mad.

"Limp-winged!" somebody said in an un-Christian
voice.

They chased her on out of the church house. Out across the weed field like a carnival of people chasing a getting-away kite. They ran her under the full moon, under the crows shadowing and cawing above them and on into the woods. She disappeared right through a grove of white oak and yellow pines. The last thing Daniel saw was Zelma's left foot, looking like a wing, as she slipped farther into the piney woods.

The people stopped right at the lush wildness, which was a curtain of green forest pulled like a secret against the place where unknown lakes and streams flowed and where wild foxes and all sorts of untamed creatures roamed.

Daniel was the only one who could have followed her there into the wildness, for he knew wild places like the back of his hand. But the look Zelma had shot him had said No.

And then he remembered that the piney woods was a natural bird refuge. There also doves flew in the thicket, marsh hens strutted proud, and quail called across the muddy and winding Sweet Earth River. He saw Zelma trembling there among the white and golden lilies and the singing crows. And Daniel knew this red earth of willow trees, dogwoods, and redbuds could hypnotize a person like Zelma who had wings in her feet, until it would be difficult for her to leave its allure.

As the church people ended their chase, he also

stopped. It seemed as if she had been gone for weeks already. But instead of following her, he did the best thing: He turned back with the others.

Mother Augusta now raised her trembling hand and directed the choir to sing Zelma's favorite number, "Lord, Just a Little Mercy's All I Need," which they began singing softly, and she conducted the song so that it slowed down to a soothing pace. Finally the Louisiana choir dispersed, gathered their belongings, got on board and continued their sweet, wafting music on the midnight bus as they started out for home and Louisiana.

"She'll be back," Mother Augusta promised Daniel, who was sitting by the altar, head sadly bowed, looking long-faced, sifting the sawdust through his fingers, sawdust Zelma Lee Moses made rise by pounding the oak into powder while doing one of her gospel-skipping holy dances.

"She'll be back," Mother Augusta repeated in a knowing voice, then added as she took apart the launching platform, "This church is full of God's grace and mercy. Zelma's seen to that." She was remembering Zelma's invisible flight of the soul every time she looked at Daniel.

"When?" asked Daniel in that deep baritone voice.

"In three days," Mother Augusta answered, mumbling something about God making humans just a little bit lower than the angels.

"Being a little spryer than a timeworn woman, she didn't know she couldn't fly," sighed Mother Augusta. "Yet we hear her flying every Sunday morning on the radio."

"Well then why did the people come if they knew she couldn't fly?" asked Daniel, forgetting the miracle of the sawdust in his hand and the clef notes in the wood he chopped that radio afternoon when Zelma's first record came over the airwaves.

"Listen," said Mother Augusta.

"I'm listening."

"They came for the same reason they got mad," answered Mother Augusta. "They didn't want to miss it just in case she could." The elderly woman paused, then added, "When she realizes she already can fly, she'll be back. Take a lesson from the crow. Why should a bird brag about flying—that jet bird just spreads two easy wings. When Zelma knows that lesson, and she will know it, she'll return, she'll sure enough return."

The next day the women gathered in the morning pews and Mother Augusta offered up a prayer of early thanks.

The deacons joined in, serving the women broom-wheat tea, gathering the cloth to help the sisters in the sanctuary sew a new gown fit for a child of God.

Somebody started lining a hymn.

It started out as a low moan.

Then it grew until it was full to bursting.

It exploded and the right word dropped from a mouth, scooted along the floor, lifted its head, flapped in place, flew up and became a note hanging from the light bulb in the rafters of the church.

A moan. A lyric.

And it went on like that, from moan to lyric.

Until the song was fully realized.

Three long days passed with the people sitting, waiting, sewing, singing.

Mother Augusta was lining a hymn and she was lining a hem.

And on the third day, and on the third day they heard the crows gathering around the church.

But they did not open their beaks.

The hymn stopped, circled the light bulb above their heads.

The sound of silence.

The sound of waiting.

Then the next sound they heard was the door of the church opening softly.

"Who is it?" Daniel asked.

"Sh!" Mother Augusta whispered.

Nobody turned around except the waiting silence.

The silence stood up and opened its welcome arms.

Zelma.

Zelma Lee.

Zelma Lee Moses.

On the third day Zelma Lee Moses, looking a little down at the heel, stepped through Perfect Peace, paused and put on her long sanctified robe of invisible wings, picked up her guitar, mounted the steps to the pulpit, opened her mouth, and began to sing a crescendo passage in a higher voice with light wings glittering in the fire-singed notes, "Lord, just a little mercy's all I need."

And she looked at Daniel with a look that some folks claimed she got from talking to the devil for three days. But this was not true.

The look was all mixed up with angels, mockingbird flights, burnished butterflies, and tree-skimming kites.

After the service Daniel took her hand and held it longer than friendly.

When Zelma glanced up at the crucifix it seemed to her that Jesus, through a divine transformation, was winking through His pain. Or maybe it was just the effect of the morning sun kindling His expression, beaming only on those muscles of the mouth that brightened the corners of His lips.

As they left the church they walked under the crucifix over the doorway.

As if he too saw the same expression on the Christ, Daniel squeezed Zelma Lee's hand tighter. And she could feel electricity pulse back and forth from his fingers to hers.

*   *   *

And they flew away to a place where wings grew from their ribs.

And they were standing still flying.

FIRST LOVE

Gary Soto

Alfonso sat on the porch trying to push his crooked teeth to where he thought they belonged. He hated the way he looked. Last week he did a hundred sit-ups a day, thinking that he would burn those already apparent ripples on his stomach to even deeper ripples, dark ones, so when he went swimming at the canal next summer, girls in cutoffs would notice. And the guys would think he was tough, someone who could take a punch and give it back. He wanted "cuts" like those he had seen on a calendar of an Aztec warrior standing on a pyramid with a woman in his arms (Even she had "cuts" he could see beneath her thin dress). The calendar hung above the cash register at La Plaza. Orsua, the owner, said he could have the calendar at the end of year if the waitress, Yolanda, didn't take it first.

Alfonso studied the magazine pictures of rock stars for a hairstyle. He liked the way Prince looked—and the bass player from Los Lobos. Alfonso thought he would look cool with his hair razored into a V in the back and streaked purple. But he knew his mother wouldn't go for it. And his father, who was *puro Mexicano,* would sit in his chair after work, sullen as a toad, and call him "sissy."

Alfonso didn't dare color his hair. But he had it butched on the top, like in the magazine. His father came home that evening from a softball game, happy that his team had drilled four homers in a 13-to-5 bashing of Color Tile. He swaggered into the living room, but stopped cold when he saw Alfonso and asked, not joking, but with real concern, "Did you hurt your head at school? *¿Que pasó?*"

Alfonso pretended not to hear his father and went to his room, where he studied his hair from all angles in the mirror. He liked what he saw until he smiled and realized, as if for the first time, that his teeth were crooked, like a pile of wrecked cars. He grew depressed and turned away from the mirror. He sat on his bed and leafed through the rock magazine until he came to the rock star with the butched top. His mouth was closed, but Alfonso was sure his teeth weren't crooked.

Alfonso didn't want to be the handsomest kid at school, but he was determined to be better-looking than average. The next day he spent his lawn-mowing money on a new shirt, and, with a pocket knife, scooped moons of dirt from under his fingernails.

He spent hours in front of the mirror trying to herd

his teeth into place with his thumb. He asked his mother if he could have braces, like Frankie Molina, her godson, but he asked at the wrong time. She was at the kitchen table licking the envelope to the house payment. She glared up at him. "Do you think money grows on trees?"

His mother clipped coupons from magazines and newspapers, kept a vegetable garden in the summer, and shopped at J. C. Penney's and K Mart. Their family ate a lot of *frijoles*, which was okay because nothing else tasted so good, although one time Alfonso had had Chinese pot stickers and thought they were the next best food in the world.

He didn't ask his mother for braces again, even when she was in a better mood, and decided to fix his teeth by pushing on them with his thumbs. After breakfast that Saturday he went to his room, closed the door quietly, turned the radio on, and pushed for three hours straight.

He pushed for ten minutes, rested for five, and every half hour, during a radio commercial, checked to see if his smile had improved. It hadn't.

Eventually he grew bored and went outside with an old gym sock to wipe down his bike, a ten-speed from Montgomery Ward. His thumbs were tired and wrinkled and pink, the way they got when he stayed in the bathtub too long.

Alfonso's older brother, Ernie, rode up on *his* Montgomery Ward bicycle looking depressed. He parked his bike against the peach tree and sat on the back steps, keeping his head down and stepping on ants that came too close.

Alfonso knew better than to say anything when Ernie looked mad. He turned his bike over, balancing it on the handlebars and seat, and flossed the spokes with the sock. When he was finished, he pressed a knuckle to his teeth until they tingled.

Ernie groaned and said, "Ah, man."

Alfonso waited a few minutes before asking, "What's the matter?" He pretended not to be too interested. He picked up a wad of steel wool and continued cleaning the spokes.

Ernie hesitated, not sure if Alfonso would laugh. But it came out. "Those girls didn't show up. And you better not laugh."

"What girls?"

Then Alfonso remembered his brother bragging about how he and Frostie met two girls from Kings Canyon Junior High last week on Halloween night. They were dressed as gypsies, the costume for all poor Chicanas—they just had to borrow scarves and gaudy-red lipstick from their *abuelitas*.

Alfonso walked over to his brother. He compared their two bikes: His gleamed like a handful of dimes while Ernie's looked dirty.

"They said we were supposed to wait at the corner. But they didn't show up. Me and Frostie waited and waited like *pendejos*. They were playing games with us."

Alfonso thought that was a pretty dirty trick but sort of funny too. He would have to try that someday.

"Were they cute?" Alfonso asked.

"I guess so."

"Do you think you could recognize them?"

"If they were wearing red lipstick, maybe."

Alfonso sat with his brother in silence, both of them smearing ants with their floppy high tops. Girls could sure act weird, especially the ones you met on Halloween.

Later that day, Alfonso sat on the porch pressing on his teeth. Press, relax; press, relax. His portable radio was on, but not loud enough to make Mr. Rojas come down the steps and wave his cane at him.

Alfonso's father drove up. Alfonso could tell by the way he sat in his truck, a Datsun with a different-colored front fender, that his team had lost their softball game. Alfonso got off the porch in a hurry because he knew his father would be in a bad mood. He went to the backyard, where he unlocked his bike, sat on it with the kickstand down, and pressed on his teeth. He punched himself in the stomach, and growled, "Cuts." Then he patted his butch and whispered, "Fresh."

After a while Alfonso pedaled up the street, hands in his pockets, toward Foster Freeze, where he was chased by a ratlike chihuahua. At his old school, John Burroughs Elementary, he found a kid hanging upside down on the top of a barbed wire fence with a girl looking up at him. Alfonso skidded to a stop and helped the kid untangle his pants from the barbed wire. The kid was grateful. He had been afraid he would have to stay up there all night. His sister, who was Alfonso's age, was also grateful. If she had to go home and tell her mother that Frankie was stuck on a fence and couldn't get down, she would get scolded.

"Thanks," she said. "What's your name?"

Alfonso remembered her from his school and noticed that she was kind of cute, with ponytails and straight teeth. "Alfonso. You go to my school, huh?"

"Yeah. I've seen you around. You live nearby?"

"Over on Madison."

"My uncle used to live on that street, but he moved to Stockton."

"Stockton's near Sacramento, isn't it?"

"You been there?"

"No." Alfonso looked down at his shoes. He wanted to say something clever the way people do on TV. But the only thing he could think to say was that the governor lived in Sacramento. As soon as he shared this observation, he winced inside.

Alfonso walked with the girl and the boy as they started for home. They didn't talk much. Every few steps, the girl, whose name was Sandra, would look at him out of the corner of her eye, and Alfonso would look away. He learned that she was in seventh grade, just like him, and that she had a pet terrier named Queenie. Her father was a mechanic at Rudy's Speedy Repair, and her mother was a teacher's aide at Jefferson Elementary.

When they came to the street, Alfonso and Sandra stopped at her corner, but her brother ran home. Alfonso watched him stop on the front yard to talk to a lady he guessed was their mother. She was raking leaves into a pile.

"I live over there," she said, pointing.

Alfonso looked over her shoulder for a long time, trying to muster enough nerve to ask her if she'd like to go bike riding tomorrow.

Shyly, he asked: "You wanna go bike riding?"

"Maybe." She played with a ponytail and crossed one leg in front of the other. "But my bike has a flat."

"I can get my brother's bike. He won't mind."

She thought a moment before she said, "Okay. But not tomorrow. I have to go to my aunt's."

"How about after school on Monday?"

"I have to take care of my brother until my mom comes home from work. How 'bout four thirty?"

"Okay," he said. "Four thirty." Instead of parting immediately, they talked for a while, asking questions like: "Who's your favorite group?" "Have you ever been on the Big Dipper at Santa Cruz?" and "Have you ever tasted pot stickers?" But the question-and-answer period ended when Sandra's mother called her home.

Alfonso took off as fast he could on his bike, jumped the curb, and cool as he could be, raced away with his hands stuffed in his pockets. But when he looked back over his shoulder, the wind raking through his butch, Sandra wasn't even looking. She was already on her lawn, heading for the porch.

That night he took a bath, pampered his hair into place, and did more than his usual set of exercises. In bed, in between the push-and-rest on his teeth, he pestered his brother to let him borrow his bike.

"Come on, Ernie," he whined. "Just for an hour."

"*Chale*, I might want to use it."

"Come on, man, I'll let you have my trick-or-treat candy."

"What you got?"

"Three baby Milky Ways and some Skittles."

"Who's going to use it?"

Alfonso hesitated, then risked the truth. "I met this girl. She doesn't live too far."

Ernie rolled over on his stomach and stared at the outline of his brother, whose head was resting on his elbow. "*You* got a girlfriend?"

"She ain't my girlfriend, just a girl."

"What does she look like?"

"Like a girl."

"Come on, what does she look like?"

"She's got ponytails and a little brother."

"Ponytails! Those girls who messed with Frostie and me had ponytails. Is she cool?"

"I think so."

Ernie sat up in bed. "I bet you that's her."

Alfonso felt his stomach knot up. "She's going to be my girlfriend, not yours!"

"I'm going to get even with her!"

"You better not touch her," Alfonso snarled, throwing a wadded Kleenex at him. "I'll run you over with my bike."

For the next hour, until their mother threatened them from the living room to be quiet or else, they argued whether it was the same girl who had stood Ernie up. Alfonso said over and over that she was too nice to pull a stunt like that. But Ernie argued that she lived only two blocks from where those girls had told them to wait, that she was in the same grade, and, the clincher, that she had ponytails. Secretly, however, Ernie was jealous that his brother, two years younger than himself, might have found a girlfriend.

Sunday morning, Ernie and Alfonso stayed away from each other, though over breakfast they fought over the last tortilla. Their mother, sewing at the kitchen table, let her eyes grow big and warned them to knock it off. At church they made faces at one another when the priest, Father Jerry, wasn't looking. Ernie punched Alfonso in the arm, and Alfonso, his eyes wide with anger, punched back.

Monday morning they hurried to school on their bikes, neither saying a word though they rode side by side. In first period, Alfonso worried himself sick. How would he borrow a bike for her? He considered asking his second best friend, Raul, for his bike. But Alfonso knew Raul, a paper boy with dollar signs in his eyes, would charge him, and he had less than sixty cents, counting the soda bottles he could cash.

Between history and math, Alfonso saw Sandra and her girl friend huddling at their lockers. He hurried by without being seen.

During lunch Alfonso hid in metal shop so he wouldn't run into Sandra. What would he say to her? If he weren't mad at his brother, he could ask Ernie what girls and guys talk about. But he *was* mad, and anyway, Ernie was pitching nickels with his friends.

Alfonso hurried home after school. He did the morning dishes as his mother had asked and raked the leaves. After finishing his chores, he did a hundred sit-ups, pushed on his teeth until they hurt, showered, and combed his hair into a perfect butch. He then stepped out to the patio to clean his bike. On an impulse, he removed the chain to wipe off the gritty oil. But while he was unhooking it from the back sprocket, it snapped. The chain lay in his hand like a dead snake.

Alfonso couldn't believe his luck. Now, not only did he not have an extra bike for Sandra, he had no bike for himself. What a mess. Frustrated, and on the verge of tears, he flung the chain as far as he could. It landed with a hard slap against the back fence and spooked his sleeping cat, Benny. Benny looked around, blinking his soft gray eyes, and went back to sleep.

Alfonso retrieved the chain, which was hopelessly broken. He cursed himself for being stupid, yelled at his bike for being cheap, and slammed the chain onto the cement. The chain snapped in another place and hit him when it popped up, slicing his hand like a snake's fang.

"Ow!" he cried, his mouth immediately going to his hand to suck on the wound.

After a dab of iodine, which only made his cut hurt more, and a lot of thought, he went to the bedroom to plead to Ernie, who was changing to his after-school clothes.

"Come on, man, let me use it," Alfonso pleaded. "Please, Ernie, I'll do anything."

Although Ernie could see Alfonso's desperation, he had plans with his friend Raymundo. They were going to catch frogs at the Mayfair Canal. Ernie felt sorry for his brother, and gave him a stick of gum to make him feel better, but there was nothing he could do. The canal was three miles away, and the frogs were waiting.

Alfonso took the stick of gum, placed it in his shirt pocket, and left the bedroom with his head down. He went outside, slamming the screen door behind him, and sat in the alley behind his house. A sparrow landed in the weeds, and when it tried to come close, Alfonso screamed for it to scram. The sparrow responded with a squeaky chirp and flew away.

At four, he decided to get it over with and started walking to Sandra's house, trudging slowly, as if he were waist deep in water. Shame colored his face. How could he disappoint his first date? She would probably laugh. She might even call him *menso*!

He stopped at the corner where they were supposed to meet and watched her house. But there was no one outside, only a rake leaning against the steps.

Why did he have to take the chain off, he scolded himself. He always messed things up when he tried to take them apart, like the time he tried to repad his baseball mitt. He had unlaced the mitt and filled the pocket with bird feathers. But when he tried to put it back together, he had forgotten how it laced up.

Everything became tangled like kite string. When he showed the mess to his mother, who was at the stove cooking dinner, she scolded him but put it back together and didn't tell his father what a dumb thing he had done.

Now he had to face Sandra and say, "I broke my bike, and my stingy brother took off on his."

He waited at the corner a few minutes, hiding behind a hedge for what seemed like forever. Just as he was starting to think about going home, he heard footsteps and knew it was too late. His hands, moist from worry, hung at his sides, and a thread of sweat raced down his armpit.

He peeked through the hedge. She was wearing a sweater with a checkerboard pattern. A red purse was slung over her shoulder. He could see her looking for him, almost tiptoeing to see if he was coming around the corner.

What have I done? Alfonso thought. He bit his lip, called himself *menso,* and pounded his palm against his forehead. Someone slapped the back of his head. He turned around and saw Ernie.

"We got the frogs, Alfonso," he said, holding up a wiggling plastic bag. "I'll show you later."

Ernie looked through the hedge, with one eye closed, at the girl. "She's not the one who messed with Frostie and me," he said finally. "You still wanna borrow my bike?"

Alfonso couldn't believe his luck. What a brother! What a pal! He promised to take Ernie's turn next time it was his turn to do the dishes. Ernie hopped on Raymundo's handlebars and said he would remember that promise. Then he was gone as they took off without looking back.

Free of worry now that his brother had come through, Alfonso emerged from behind the hedge with Ernie's bike, which was mud-splashed but better than nothing. Sandra waved.

"Hi," she said.

"Hi," he said back.

She looked cheerful. Alfondo told her his bike was broken and asked if she wanted to ride with him.

"Sounds good," she said, and jumped on the cross-bar.

It took all of Alfonso's strength to steady the bike. He started off slowly, gritting his teeth, because she was heavier than he thought. But once he got going, it got easier. He pedaled smoothly, sometimes with only one hand on the handlebars, as they sped up one street and down another. Whenever he ran over a pothole, which was often, she screamed with delight, and once, when it looked like they were going to crash, she placed her hand over his, and it felt like love.

AFTER THE WAR

Jeanne Wakatsuki Houston

As the crowd gathered around the taunting gladiators, Reiko ran in the opposite direction, fear of violence beating a drum in her chest. That's when she bumped into Sara, so hard Sara's glasses were knocked off. Both were running away from the mob around Willie Jackson and Peter Novak, who were warming up to a fist fight.

"Nigger, I'm gonna make you eat dirt!" shouted Pete, a new sixth-grade student from Chicago.

"Shut up, polack! You gonna eat dirt and them words!" Willie had been king of the school, a sleek panther reigning over the jungle playground, until the newcomer from the East had come to challenge him.

Reiko was afraid of Willie. She was sure he was a demon. Her grandmother had told her demons hid in the human body and were invisible except for certain signs—like fire that escaped from the feet and mouth. Willie stalked across the playground in his shiny cordovan shoes, scraping metal taps on his heels against the asphalt. Sparks flew from them like fireworks, and sometimes flaming threats blasted from his mouth. She stayed as far away from him as she could.

"I'm really sorry," said Reiko. "I didn't see you." She picked up the plastic-rimmed glasses and handed them to Sara.

Reiko had seen Sara at school and around the housing project where they both lived, but they never had exchanged words. That wasn't saying much, because Reiko hardly spoke to anyone. She was shy and had moved to Cabrillo Homes only a month before. Before that she had lived in a Japanese-American internment camp for three years, from 1942 to 1945.

Surprising herself, she continued, "I'm Reiko. You live around the corner from me in the two-story apartments, don't you? And you have a younger brother named Alden."

With glasses on, Sara's eyes magnified like an owl's. Her pursed lips beaked over protruding front teeth. She stared at Reiko, her expression serious, yet friendly.

"My name is Sara. You've just moved here, haven't you?"

Reiko had learned to recognize the Southern and Midwestern accents of people living in the housing project. Sara's was different. A strange nasal twang rang in her voice. Her face also seemed different—

soft and scared compared to the freckled toughness of girls like Doris Jean Hall and Billie May Thorne, who were from Texas and swore at boys.

Sara smiled widely, exposing buck teeth. "Shall we walk home together? I don't want to see the fight, do you?"

"No. Those guys scare me even when they're *not* fighting. Let's go." Reiko could hear yelling, and then a shrill whistle screeched. Thank God, a teacher had arrived.

On the walk home Reiko learned Sara was from Boston. Her parents had come to California in 1943 during the war to work in the shipyards. After the war ended and the plants were shut down, they remained and continued to live in the government project.

"Where did you live before you moved here?" asked Sara.

"In a place called Poston . . . in Arizona." Reiko was uneasy. She didn't know how to explain about the internment camps and was relieved when Sara accepted her answer without further questions. She had left out the part about living in a trailer camp in Lomitas for six months until a social worker had placed her family in Cabrillo Homes.

Reiko was glad finally to talk to someone, to have a friend. Even though Sara was younger and different from the other kids—making her as much an outsider as she was—Reiko was elated. They parted warmly, promising to meet the next day.

But Sara was absent from school the rest of the week. Reiko wondered if she was sick. She was too shy to visit . . . and afraid Sara's parents might not approve of a friendship with a Japanese girl. Instead, she folded three cranes from white origami paper and waited to give them the following Monday. Her grandmother had said cranes were good luck and inspired long life.

That Saturday during breakfast, a tentative knock sounded on Reiko's front door, which opened into the kitchen. She and her brother and sister were sitting at the table eating warmed-up chow mein. Reiko opened the door and was shocked to see Sara's large-toothed and smiling face. Quickly she stepped outside and closed it behind her, embarrassed Sara might have seen them eating chow mein for breakfast.

"Can you come for a ride with us today? My dad said it was all right to ask you." Sara did not look like someone recovering from sickness. She was bright and bouncy.

"A ride?" Reiko was not familiar with this kind of recreation.

"Yeah. A car ride. It's lots of fun. Can you come?"

Since both her mother and father worked at the fish cannery, even on Saturdays, Reiko would have to ask permission from her grandmother. She reentered the house, leaving Sara outside waiting.

"Ba-chan, can I go for a ride with my friends?"

Ba-chan's eagle eyes pierced her. "What kind ride to where?"

"Just to town," she fibbed.

Ba-chan kept peering, looking like she could see through her. Reiko didn't know Ba-chan's exact age. Her body was tiny and spry, her unlined face framed by white hair swept up into a bun. She looked young, but Reiko figured she was between seventy and a hundred. She was very wise and couldn't be fooled.

"Okay. But no boys. No come home late."

She grabbed her jacket and the three origami cranes, which she gave to Sara. Sara was delighted, having never seen folded origami paper before, and when Reiko told her they were for good luck and long life, she seemed even more impressed.

A tall man with curly dark hair stood beside a black Packard sedan parked next to Sara's apartment building. Alden, Sara's nine-year-old brother, was jumping up and down on the running board.

"Okay, Babe, ready to go?" the man called cheerfully.

"Daddy, this is my friend Reiko."

"How d'you do," he said, smiling broadly, and held out a large hand.

Lost inside his bear paw, her hand felt like a new-born baby chick. His firm, warm grasp felt odd. She realized she had never shaken a white man's hand before.

"How do you do," she answered politely. "Thank you for inviting me."

"Hey . . ." His eyes were wide. "You speak English pretty good!"

Reiko wasn't offended. She had learned quickly, soon after she enrolled in school, that it surprised kids she spoke English and could read and write so well— in most cases better than they did. She hadn't learned yet how to explain she too had been born in America and knew no other language but English. She couldn't speak Japanese and understood only bits and pieces when her grandmother talked.

After some bickering between Sara and Alden about who was to sit in the front seat next to Mr. Bowen, it was decided everyone would take turns. The backseat of the Packard was roomy with velvety felt seats as big as a sofa. To Reiko it was luxurious. Her father's car was an old, worn Chevy that didn't start most of the time.

Once they were on the Pacific Coast Highway, Mr. Bowen yelled, "Which way shall we go? South to Winchester? Or north to Santa Monica?" All the windows were rolled down and the wind whipped through the car, blowing his hair into a wiry halo.

"Santa Monica!" they shouted together.

"Here we go!" he yelled again, stepping on the gas so that the car lunged forward like a bronco. Reiko and Sara bounced against the front seats, laughing hysterically.

"I'm an old cowhand . . . from the Rio Grande," sang Mr. Bowen. "And my legs ain't bold . . . and my cheeks ain't crammed." His ad-libbed lyrics drove them further into paroxysms and while he sang "Yip-pee-yai-yo-kai-yay," he continued to jerk the car as if it were a reticent stallion.

Reiko felt she had entered another world, a roller-coaster world of laughter, noise, and craziness. During the last few months in the Arizona internment camp, she had dreaded reentering "American" life. Her world for three years had been one of Asian faces and close family ties. What was life among the whites going to be like? And now this wild introduction was enchanting! It was fun! Mr. Bowen was a jovial bear, a loud Santa Claus! He had heavy jowls and a thick neck, and his stomach strained against the buttons of his plaid shirt. Her grandmother would say he was *hotei-san*, the fat god of happiness.

They drove and drove, down the highway, through alleys and side streets, and all the while he sang, told jokes and stories, and lectured. Once they parked outside the airport and watched planes land, and whenever one took off, he sang, "Off we go, into the wild blue yonder, flying high . . . into the sky."

"I used to be a pilot," he said. "Flying's a helluva lot safer than driving. Wish I were still up there. It's the closest to God you can get."

In his nasal Boston accent he talked to them all as equals, as if they were intimate friends. Reiko wanted to ask him why he didn't fly anymore, but felt somehow it was not a polite question. During most of the ride she said nothing. She was mesmerized by him, amazed that any father could be so much fun. Her own was quiet and serious. He was kind, but rarely showed humor or frivolity, and would never consider taking a day to drive his children around the countryside for entertainment. She envied Sara.

After an ice cream cone treat at Ocean Park, they headed back to Long Beach. It had been a long day. The black Packard eased into its parking space. It was early evening and the brilliant orange sky was tinged with lavender. For the first time, Reiko wondered about Sara's mother.

"Is she home? She won't mind that we've been gone so long?" Reiko knew her own mother would have been anxious, and she wasn't looking forward to the scolding she knew Ba-chan would give when she got home.

There was a moment of strained silence as Sara avoided her eyes.

"My mom worked today," she said quickly. "At the drugstore next to Cole's Market."

Reiko understood this. Her parents always worked on weekends too. As they walked past the apartment's dark, curtained windows, she imagined Mrs. Bowen setting a lace-covered table with silver and candles, heaping porcelain plates with meat and mashed potatoes and lemon meringue pie while Glenn Miller's "In the Mood" played on the radio.

She thanked Mr. Bowen. "Anytime, Ray-Ray," he said cheerily. Alden jumped on his back diverting his attention, and the conversation ended. Reiko was disappointed. She wanted to shake his bear paw one more time.

Reiko and Sara became close friends. They walked to school together and ate lunch at the edge of the grounds, far away from where the tough kids hung out. Reiko taught her how to fold origami paper and draw pictures of flowers and pretty girls . . . all blue-eyed blondes and redheads. They filled notebooks with ballerinas, ice-skaters, princesses and queens wearing diamond-studded tiaras.

On weekends, sometimes on both Saturday and Sunday, the bucking sedan galloped to new outposts—Downey, Norwalk, Anaheim, Redondo Beach, Venice, and Glendale. Reiko grew to love Mr. Bowen, his large belly that shook when he laughed, his bulbous nose lined by fine hairnet purple webs. She looked forward to weekends and the long drives. Some days they never stopped, but kept on going, one continuous ride through town after town after town.

Though Reiko began to feel as close to Sara as she did to her own sister, she never invited her into the house. She was afraid Sara would find the meager furnishings and food smells strange, even distasteful. Grandma insisted on saving everything—paper bags, strings, rags, jars. She bundled them all neatly in balls and packages, but they filled the closets and shelves, overflowing into cardboard boxes that lined the walls of the kitchen and living room. And pervading everything were the salty smells of *tsukemono*—fermented vegetables—and pungent fish drying in one of the bedrooms.

Nor did Sara ever invite Reiko into her apartment. Reiko figured it was because the Bowens were private—being from Boston and high-toned, owning a Packard sedan. She also surmised it was "upper-class" white people whose fathers entertained their kids. She was embarrassed even to introduce Sara to her father, afraid he wouldn't even smile!

One day as they walked home from school, Sara surprised her. "Would you like to meet my mom? We could stop by the drugstore."

"Oh, yes!" said Reiko, controlling excitement. She was even a little nervous. They walked along Santa

Fe Highway to a small shop cluttered with magazines, cosmetics, colognes, medicines, candy, and even some liquor. A thin woman stood behind one of the counters.

"Hi, Mom," said Sara.

The woman smiled, narrow face brightening. "Well, hi, honey. What a nice surprise." She looked at Reiko warmly. "This must be your friend. Hi, honey."

Reiko's heart melted at the woman's friendliness. Although the sallow complexion and peakedness didn't fit her imagined picture of an elegant hostess in a ruffled apron, she was awed. Her accent was clipped, and her face was heavily made up with bright rouge that stood out from her cheeks like pink fifty-cent pieces.

"Anything special you want, honey?" she asked Sara.

"Oh, no, Mom. I just wanted you to meet Reiko."

Sara was studying her mother's face, whose eyes were dark, almost beady, and seemed to glitter. For a moment Reiko sensed sadness passing between them.

"Here's some candy, dahlings," she said and handed them two Hershey bars. "I loved meeting you, Ricky." To Reiko's astonishment she came from behind the counter and kissed her cheek, trailing a sweet scent of perfume and tobacco.

"Now, you two get going. I'll see you in a while, Sara."

Walking home, Reiko was in a daze. How different Sara's parents were from hers. She couldn't imagine her mother kissing her in public . . . let alone a friend! And to be called "honey" and "dahling."

The following Saturday Sara came over promptly at nine. Reiko was waiting with a packed lunch. She had asked her grandmother if she could take something to show her appreciation for the rides. Grandma always said never to go to someone's house empty-handed . . . even if all you had to give was a can of tomatoes or peaches. When Grandma offered to make lunch, Reiko wanted to decline, worrying she would make rice balls and *tsukemono*. Ba-chan probably guessed this because she said, "No worry. I make sando-witchie . . . *hakujin* [Caucasian] kind. Okay? No *kussai* [smelly] things."

Inside the felt-lined Packard Reiko felt cozy and at home. As they sped along the highway toward Huntington Beach, Mr. Bowen rambled on about movie stars.

"Frances Langford worked in a fruit stand where I used to buy apples. She really could croon a tune. . . even then. And Betty Grable was a carhop before she made it in the movies. She waited on me once."

Alden and Reiko, whose turn it was to be in the

back, stood leaning against the front seat, ears recording every word.

"And Franchot Tone . . . he was a hairdresser."

"Daddy, did you really know those stars?" Alden asked.

"Hell yes! I knew 'em. I drove taxi, remember? I guess you wouldn't. Hell, yes, I knew 'em. Drove them everywhere . . . the Grauman's Chinese, the Palladium, Lick Pier."

They stopped at a beach and ate Ba-chan's lunch. Reiko was proud of the American fare—tuna sandwiches, potato chips, boiled eggs, and fresh pears.

"This is delicious, Ray-Ray," Mr. Bowen said. "Your grandma can cook for me anytime."

Early evening, and the shiny sedan pulled into its parking stall, choking and sputtering from its pull over long asphalt trails. The four weary explorers tumbled out. As they walked past the draped windows of the apartment, a loud crash and sounds of tinkling glass jarred the quiet dusk. Mr. Bowen ran to the front door. He fumbled at the lock and began shouting, "Emily! Emily! For God's sake, what's happening!"

Alden and Sara froze on the sidewalk, staring at their father. He unlocked the door and disappeared, leaving it ajar so Reiko could see the kitchen sink inside. It was getting dark, but not enough to hide a mound of dirty dishes piled on the counter.

Sara grabbed her hand and whispered, "I'm scared. Please come in with me."

Alden was whimpering. As they entered, Reiko saw their kitchen was very much like hers—ice box, small gas stove, sink with a wooden counter, flowered linoleum on the floor. Open cereal boxes, an uncapped milk bottle, and bowls half-filled with soggy corn-flakes were scattered over a red Formica table. No lace tablecloth or baskets of freshly baked cookies.

The kitchen opened onto the living room, which was dark draped and carpeted with a braided rag rug. A huge couch and two stuffed chairs filled the small space. It reminded Reiko of the upholstered backseat of the Packard, musty and velvet lined. Newspapers were strewn about and several ashtrays overflowed with cigarette butts. She wished Mr. Bowen would begin singing, or a wind would blow away the heavy curtains, breathing in light and air, cutting away the stale tobacco smell.

Sara's hand squeezed hers as they walked into the living room. Alden remained sniveling by the sink. Through an open door, Reiko saw Mrs. Bowen's nightgowned figure standing unsteadily in front of a cracked full-length mirror. In her hand were the jagged remains of a broken bottle. Shards of mirror glittered on the carpet amidst several empty pints and fifths.

"Emily honey, please put that down. Don't hurt

yourself, please." Mr. Bowen's voice was unfamiliarly soft.

Mrs. Bowen's eyes were black from smudged mascara, and Reiko could see gray rivulets running down her cheeks.

Weaving, she pointed the broken bottle at her distorted reflection in the mirror. "I hate you, you goddamn drunk," she slurred. "You no-good bitch!"

"You're okay, honey. Everything's okay. Just give me the bottle."

She screamed, "Matt! I can't stand it anymore. I want to die! Every weekend! I can't stop! Kill me! Kill me!"

"Just hand over the bottle, Emily." His voice was pleading.

A sadness for Mr. Bowen swept over Reiko. Her eyes began to burn and her throat ached. She wished his bear shouts would rattle the apartment, just as they had shaken the insides of the Packard.

"Oh, God, please help me. Help me, Matt." She dropped the bottle and collapsed in his arms.

"There, there, baby, it's okay. It's okay." As the door closed, his soothing voice almost crooned.

Sara's owl eyes studied Reiko's. They were no longer frightened, just sad. Reiko remembered the moment between Sara and her mother at the drugstore. She realized she was now privy to that look, the look of a well-kept secret. She felt her throat tighten. She would keep Sara's secret and was determined not to cry.

"I'll meet you at the corner," Reiko said lightly as she walked through the kitchen to leave. "Same time Monday morning."

Monday they walked to school as if nothing had passed over the weekend. Inwardly, Reiko felt things were not the same, but she couldn't describe what had changed. Her friendship with Sara was intact, even stronger. But something was different within herself.

They met for lunch as usual and were chattering about funny books, when a commotion began on the softball field. Another battle between Willie and Pete. They could hear the shouts.

"Hit me, lard-ass, if you're man enough," yelled Willie.

"You're not getting off this time, nigger-sissy," Pete shouted back. "No teacher's going to stop me now!"

Instead of drawing away from the kids hurrying to surround the fighters, Reiko found herself running to join them. Sara was close behind. Feeling no fear, Reiko was surprised. She was now curious, unthreatened by the impending violence.

By the time they reached the arena, fists were flying, and the sickening thuds of knuckles against cheekbone

accentuated the bellows and curses. Dust thickened
the air, and through its haze, Reiko saw Willie's
clenched dragon claws battering Pete until he fell.

Suddenly, Pete screamed. "My leg! My leg! It's
broken! Oh, God, it's broken!"

He was on the ground, on his back, writhing,
pounding the dirt with his fists. His large body quivered, one leg outstretched and the other twisted gro-
tesquely beneath him. Willie stood a few feet away,
silent, stunned. He stared at his fallen adversary.

A shrill whistle and Mr. Chambers, a sixth-grade
teacher, jostled his way through the crowd. Pete was
crying now, "Oh, God, my mom's going to beat me.
We don't have money for a doctor. Oh, God, she'll
kill me." He was blubbering, big tears wetting his
face.

Willie looked scared and helpless. Mr. Chambers
got the four biggest boys to bring a detached wooden
door to carry Pete to the office. Willie helped lift him
onto the stretcher, and Reiko saw him mumble something in Pete's ear. Then while the others carried him
from the field, he walked next to them and held Pete's
hand. All the time Pete was crying, "My mom's going
to kill me. Jesus-God, she'll beat my ass."

Reiko watched the entourage grow smaller as they
neared the building. Willie's cordovans were dull with
dust, no longer shooting off sparks. His dark skin had
lost the sheen of dragon scales. She wondered if the

demon had left Willie! She would have to ask Ba-chan
if a demon could ever leave someone's body.

Later, walking home with Sara, she felt hollow—
as if she had lost something. But, in another way, she
felt strong, less afraid.

She said to Sara, "Would you like to meet my
grandmother? Instead of going for a ride Saturday,
why don't you come to my house? I'll teach you to
twirl the baton."

Sara's face lit up. "Really? I didn't know you could
twirl the baton." Then she added, relief in her voice,
"That will be fun. I was getting tired of driving
around, weren't you?"

"Yeah, I was," lied Reiko. "So, come over this
Saturday and I'll start teaching you."

But that weekend Sara did not show up. Reiko was
too embarrassed to go to Sara's, afraid Mrs. Bowen
might be drunk and she would find Sara and Alden
had gone riding with Mr. Bowen again. She winced
as she thought of the boisterous bear at the wheel,
singing and shouting at the windshield as they sped
down the highways.

When Sara did not come to school the next week,
Reiko went to the Bowen apartment and found it
vacant. The curtainless windows stood out like empty
eye sockets, and trash-filled boxes sagged and crumpled against the door.

Neighbors said they had piled as much as they could into their big car and left for New Jersey. Reiko was sad Sara never said good-bye, but didn't take it personally. Sara must have had her reasons. Reiko had learned things were not always as they appeared to be, and besides, she was glad the sleek black Packard no longer had to roam the southern California roads so aimlessly. She wanted it to have a true destination.

UPSTREAM

Gerald Haslam

That morning when my Uncle Arlo Epps stalked out from the cabin buck naked, he declared, "I'm a unsheathed soul!" Then he dove right into the Kern River and swam, angling kinda upstream to fight the current so that, whenever he finally turned directly into it, he just hung in that swift water, about halfway across, straight out from where I stood watching him.

"A unsheathed soul?" I asked myself. That sounded more like some preacher than my uncle.

He sure picked a terrible place to swim, the river right there, just below where Kern Canyon opened into the southern Sierras, because that water, it was snowmelt straight from the high country, and it come down fast and freezing. Directly above where Arlo took to swimming, there was these rapids couldn't no boat get through and, at the canyon's mouth, this cataract was boiling.

At first I just stood there and watched him, stunned, I guess. Once Uncle Arlo got turned into the current, though, and chugged into a rhythm that held him even with me—slipping back, then pulling forward again—I hollered at him, "Uncle Arlo! Uncle Arlo!"

"Leave the ol' fool be," snapped Aunt Mazie Bee, leaning on the dark cabin's doorway. "He's just a-tryin' to attract attention." She disappeared back into darkness talking to herself.

Me, I spent most of that morning watching my uncle surge, slip back, then surge again, as he tried to hold even with the cabin. You know, I'd never even seen him naked before, let alone acting so crazy, so I didn't know what to do. A couple times I asked Mazie Bee if we shouldn't try to help him some way.

"Help him?" she finally huffed. "Arlo Epps is a growed man. He can just take care a hisself."

"But he might get drownded," I insisted.

"Hah!" was all she said.

I wasn't surprised at her acting so hateful toward him. They'd had an argument that morning, as usual. I'd heard them rumbling at one another through the walls. It went on longer than most and I'd begun to wonder if there'd be any breakfast at all; then he'd jumped into the river. As a matter of fact, there wasn't no breakfast, but I never really noticed because I was so worried about Uncle Arlo.

Come midafternoon, me avoiding chores to watch him fight that current, still figuring him to collapse any second, I determined to rescue my uncle. Without asking permission, I pulled our boat, the Packard Prow Special, out from the shed and dragged her to the river's bank.

The Special was this old wooden dinghy that Uncle Arlo, he'd took for a dowsing job years before. She'd never looked too great but, in spite of her one-lunged motor, he'd been able to use her on that river without no trouble. What give the Special class, though, was that Packard hood ornament Arlo'd wired to her prow. He'd traded for it at this yard sale and he kept it all the time shined, something that really ate at Aunt Mazie Bee. She said it just showed how foolish he was. She said that all the time.

Anyways, I launched the boat and managed to maneuver it into position next to my uncle, that bright ornament pointed upstream toward the canyon. I leaned over to talk to him, but was shocked by what I seen. He was so *white*. I'd always seen his arms from the elbow down, and his face, all real tan, but the rest of him—the part his clothes hid—was the color of a trout's belly, and it seemed like he shimmered in that clear, rushing water like some kinda ghost. It was scary. "Uncle Arlo," I finally called, "please come in. You'll get drownded for sure."

My uncle, he just kept on cruising, his face out of the water every other stroke. His eyes, they looked real big and white, but I couldn't tell if he recognized me. "Shall I bring you some dinner?" I yelled. "You gotta eat." He never answered, but those two-tone arms kept stretching, those white eyes turning.

Then he done something that surprised me. This fat stonefly, it come bouncing down the water toward him. Just before it reached his face, he twisted his body and snapped the big insect into his mouth. "Crime-in-ently!" I gasped. I surely wasn't gonna mention *that* to Aunt Mazie Bee.

Whenever I chugged the Packard Prow back to shore, I hurried to the cabin and confronted my aunt. "You *gotta* do something," I insisted. "Uncle Arlo'll get drownded for sure."

"He'll no such a thang," she snapped. "Arlo Epps won't act his age is what he won't. He just wants attention, but what he needs is to brang some money in this house and stop his durn dreamin'."

"But Aunt Mazie Bee—"

"No buts! Now do your chores!"

Well, I stayed up all that night, or tried to—I reckon I mighta dozed some, leaning against the Special there on the bank. Not much, though, 'cause in the moonlight I could see him, out there holding against the current, that white body almost flashing like a fishing lure, never still. Just about dawn, I snuck in the cabin and brewed coffee, then filled the old thermos bottle. I knew my uncle, he had to be froze by then and I was determined to force some hot coffee down him.

I carried it to the Special, then bucked the river's swirl out to Arlo and positioned the boat right next to him. He didn't pay me no mind. "You gotta drink some coffee," I urged. "Uncle Arlo, ple-e-ease." He kept pulling against that rushing water, snapping at the morning's hatch of mayflies. I finally give up.

That afternoon, a reporter and a photographer from the Bakersfield newspaper, they showed up. My aunt'd called them. "I thought you wasn't gonna give Uncle Arlo no attention," I hissed to her out the corner of my mouth.

"Hesh up," she snapped, "or I'll peench a chunk outta you. Besides, I'm not a-givin' him the kind he wants, I'll tell you that much. We gotta live some way, don't we?"

That reporter he was a stout gent that chewed on a unlit cigar. His partner was a little weasel lugging this big, giant camera, and with a fat bag hanging from one shoulder. He listed whenever he walked.

After my aunt got done telling her story, that reporter, he just closed his notebook and put his stub pencil away. "Lady," he said real rough, "you must think we were born yesterday. Nobody could do what you claim your old man's done. We weren't born yesterday, right, Earl?"

"Right," agreed the photographer.

"Ask the boy," snapped Mazie Bee, unwilling to back down.

The reporter, he wiggled his wet cigar at her, then he turned to face me. "Well, boy?" he demanded.

I looked at the ground. "It's true. Honest."

We was standing on the river's bank, maybe a hundred feet from where Uncle Arlo worked against the current. The reporter, he stared at that pale form that the rushing water made look like a torpedo. Then he asked, "What's that guy wearing?"

I looked at my aunt and she looked at me. "Well, he left in a big hurry," she finally said.

"Yeah, but what's he wearing?"

"Nothin,' she choked.

"Nothing? You mean he's bare-assed?"

"Yeah," I gulped, and my aunt she looked away.

"For Chrissake, Earl, get a picture of that nut!"

"Right," said the photographer.

"What'd you say his name was?" asked the reporter, and Aunt Mazie Bee, she smiled.

The story, with a picture, they was in that next morning's paper and the crowds began arriving before lunch. My aunt, she was ready for them.

Mazie Bee stationed herself at the gate in a warped wooden lawn chair we'd salvaged years before from the river. She also had me set up our old card table—that we got cheap at a yard sale—and she put on it a cigar box to hold all the money she planned to collect, plus a can to spit snuff juice into. Across her lap she laid our old single-shot .410 that Uncle Arlo'd

swapped for way back when. Finally, she tied on her
good sunbonnet and waited. "Ever'body pays,
buster," she told the first arrival. "That'll be two
bits." Then she spit into the can, *ptui!*, and give me
a I-told-you-so grin.

What a buncha jokers turned out. While my uncle
was struggling out in that water, pickups and jalopies
and hot rods sped to the fence and out spilled the
darndest specimens I ever seen: mostly young studs
with more tattoos per square mile than the state pen.
All colors and shapes, sleeves rolled up and sucking
on toothpicks, gals parading in bathing suits and
shorts, giggling and pointing while boyfriends, they
scowled at each other.

"Hell, I could swim 'er easy," claimed one old boy
that had a pack of cigarettes rolled into a sleeve of his
T-shirt, and the crowd cheered. A minute later, he
was into a fight with another guy that had his sleeves
rolled up too, and the crowd surged and tugged for
a minute, then cheered some more.

Aunt Mazie Bee hardly seemed to notice the goings-
on. She sat counting quarters and filling that spit can.
Once she called, "No rock throwin', buster," and she
gestured with her scattergun. The old boy quit fling-
ing stones at Uncle Arlo right now.

A little later, after she'd sold a couple of old tires
for a dollar and this beat-up bike seat for thirty cents,
a great big pot-bellied devil without no shirt on, he

swaggered up to the doorway of our cabin, but my aunt never blinked: "Nothin' for sale in there, buster, but you about to buy this .410 shell." She clicked back the hammer, and he lost interest in the cabin right smart. A hour later she sold the lawn chair to a Mexican man for seventy-five cents and took to accepting bids on the card table. I never liked the way she was eyeing the Packard Prow Special.

It was about dark, the crowd finally drifting off, whenever that Cadillac, it swooped up to the gate. Out of the driver's seat come this big, tough-looking guy in a suit and tie that went and opened a back door. A short, fat guy—in a suit and tie but with a hat too—he squeezed out. The two of them, they paid my aunt—by now she was sitting on a nail keg— then they trooped through what was left of the picnickers and beer drinkers, the crowd kinda opening and staring real quiet as them two passed. Those two looked like they'd showed up at the wrong place.

On the point closest to Uncle Arlo, they stood for a long time, those two, not talking to one another that I could see, their eyes on them two-tone arms, on that two-tone head, and on that ghost of a body in the current. Finally, the fat man, he called to my aunt in this high-pitched voice: "Lady, you got a boat we can use?"

Mazie Bee's eyes narrowed. "Fer what?"

"For five dollars."

He was speaking my aunt's language, so even before she answered I was trudging to the Special. I knew I'd be ferrying the fat guy. There wasn't room for three in the Special, so the fat guy's friend, he stayed on shore while the two of us chugged out, the current jerking and pushing us around till I got that hood ornament pointed upstream and we moved toward Uncle Arlo. That bigshot, he clung to the boat's sides tight as he could, and I was half temped to dump us both just to keep him away from Arlo because there was *something* about him. He didn't fit.

Whenever we finally maneuvered alongside my uncle, the fat guy, he raised one hand, signaling me to stop, then grabbed the boat's side again right away. He watched the swimmer for a long time, then rasped to me, "How long you say he's been at it, boy?"

"Over two days."

"Two days without stopping?"

"Uh-huh."

"Take me back," he ordered. "I seen enough."

Soon as we hit shore, the fat man and his pal, they joined Aunt Mazie Bee in the cabin after she give me the .410, along with orders to make sure nobody got in without paying, and not to take less than twenty cents for the nail keg. She carried the cigar box with her.

Half an hour later, my aunt walked the fat man and his pal to that Cad', shook hands, then come back to the gate as they drove away. "Well, I sold him," she announced, her hands on her hips, her chin out, grinning.

"Huh?"

"Your uncle, I sold him to that there Mr. Rattocazano of Wide World Shows. Your uncle's a-gonna be famous and we're a-gonna be rich," she told me real proud.

"But you can't *sell* Uncle Arlo," I protested. "You can't do that!"

"I can so!" she asserted. "Besides, I never exactly sold *him,* I jest sold that Mr. Rattocazano the right to exhibit him. Course, we gotta git him declared crazy first, but Mr. Rattocazano says his lawyer'll take care a that in no time. They'll brang him and the sher'ff out tomorra."

"The sheriff?"

"To declare Arlo Epps nuts and take him. He's been crazier'n a bedbug for years. Now he can finally support us."

"But Aunt Mazie Bee . . ." I complained.

"You jest hesh!" she snapped. "This here's growed-ups' business."

Tired as I was, I couldn't sleep that night for worrying about my uncle that never hurt a soul being declared nuts and took to the nuthouse or stuck in some kinda freak show. No sir, was all I could think, not to my uncle you don't. It seemed like to me that Aunt Mazie Bee was the one gone crazy.

Before dawn, I crept out to the Packard Prow Special and hit the river. Soon as the engine coughed me out alongside Uncle Arlo—him not looking any different to me than he had that first morning, arms reaching for the water in front of him, head turning regular to breathe—I hollered at him, hoping the river's growl would cover my voice. "You gotta come back, Uncle Arlo," I pleaded. "The sheriff's gonna come and take you away. They say you've went crazy." His movements never changed, so I added, "I brung a towel."

His face kept turning, his arms pulling, but I noticed his eyes roll in my direction: He seen me. We seen each other. A real look. So I told him again: "You gotta come in. The sheriff's coming today, and a lawyer too. They'll take you to the nuthouse or the sideshow, one." I extended that towel.

His body, it just shimmered in that hurried water, and his arms kept up their rhythm, but the look on his face, it changed. Then, sure as anything, he winked at me. That was when I noticed that the Special, it was gradually falling behind him. I thought for a second that the sick old motor was giving up but, no, it sounded the same as always. Then I realized that he was moving upstream, real slow but moving, toward the rapids and that cataract.

I opened the throttle of the Special and caught Arlo,

but not for long. We was getting close to those rapids, and he was moving faster all the time. Them two-tone arms, they was churning faster and his two-tone face hardly seemed to be sucking air at all as he dug in. The Special was wide open, but it was lagging farther and farther behind, so I throttled back the engine to hold even in the current, not wanting to get into the rapids.

Up ahead, I seen my uncle slide into them, kinda bounce but keep swimming, around curling whirlpools, up swooshing runs, over hidden boulders, not believing what I was seeing with my own eyes, until pretty soon he reached the boiling edge of that cataract. I couldn't hardly breath.

For what seemed like a long, long time, he disappeared in the white water and I was scared he'd finally drownded. Then I seen this pale shape shoot up outta the water, looking less like a man at this distance than some fair fish. The current, it drove him back, but a second later he come out of that froth again, farther this time, almost over the worst of it but not quite, and he fell back into that terrible foam. I figured him a goner for sure, and I squeezed my eyes closed not wanting to see what happened. A second later, I couldn't resist squinting them open. "Come *on*, Uncle Arlo," I heard myself rooting, "*make* it!"

Then he exploded, a ghost that popped from the cataract like . . . well, almost like a unsheathed soul, smack into the smooth water above. I couldn't believe it, but I cheered, "Yaaaay!"—my heart pumping like sixty. Whenever I rubbed my eyes and shook my head, he was stroking up there out of sight into the canyon.

I plopped in the wiggling Special, breathing real heavy, and I wiped my own face with the towel I'd brung for Uncle Arlo. He was away and I was exhausted, so I pointed the Packard Prow toward the bank. Whenever I got to shore, Aunt Mazie Bee come out from the cabin. "Where's your uncle at?" she demanded, her eyes searching the river.

"He drownded," I replied.

She glanced from me to the stream and back, made a clucking sound with her mouth, then said, "He *would*."

TWISTERS AND SHOUTERS

Maxine Hong Kingston

In the Tenderloin, depressed and unemployed, the jobless Wittman Ah Sing felt a kind of bad freedom. Agoraphobic on Market Street, ha ha. There was nowhere he had to be, and nobody waiting to hear what happened to him today. Fired. Aware of Emptiness now. Ha ha. A storm will blow from the ocean or down from the mountains, and knock the set of the City down. If you dart quick enough behind the stores, you'll see that they are stage flats propped up. On the other side of them is ocean forever, and the great valley between the Coast Range and the Sierras. Is that snow on Mount Shasta?

And what for had they set up Market Street? To light up the dark jut of land into the dark sea. To bisect the city diagonally with a swath of lights. We are visible. See us? We're here. Here we are.

Well, here was First Street, and the terminal. The end of the City. The end of the week. Maws—gaps and gapes—continuing to open. But Wittman did too have a place to go, he'd been invited to a party, which he'd meant to turn down. He entered the terminal, which is surrounded by a concrete whirlpool for the buses to turn around on spirals of ramps. Not earth dirt, but like cement dirt covered everything, rush-hour feet scuffing up lime, and noses and mouths inhaling lime rubbings. A last flower stand by the main entrance—chrysanthemums. And a bakeshop with birthday cakes. A couple of people were eating cream puffs as they hurried along. People eat here, with the smell of urinal cakes issuing from johns. They buy hot dogs at one end of the terminal and finish eating on their way through. They buy gifts at the last moment. Wittman bought two packs of Pall Malls in preparation for the rest of the weekend. No loiterers doing anything freaky. Keep it moving. Everybody's got a place to go tonight. Wittman bought a ticket for the Oakland-Berkeley border, and rode up the escalator to the hangar with lanes of buses. The people on traffic islands waited along safety railings. Birds came flying full tilt from the high steel rafters to land precisely at a crumb between grill bars. The pigeons and sparrows were grayish and the cheeks of men were also gray. Pigeon dust. Pigeons fan our breathing air with pigeon dander.

Wittman was one of the first passengers to board, and chose the aisle seat behind the driver, threw his coat on the window seat to discourage company, stuck his long legs out diagonally, and put on his metaphor glasses and looked out the window.

Up into the bus clambered this very plain girl, who lifted her leg in such an ungainly manner that anybody could see up her skirt to thighs but weren't interested in looking. She was carrying string bags of books and greasy butcher paper bundles and pastry boxes. He wished she weren't Chinese, the kind who works hard and doesn't fix herself up. She, of course, stood beside him until he moved his coat and let her bump her bags across him and sit herself down to ride. This girl and her roast duck will ride beside him all the way across the San Francisco-Oakland Bay Bridge. She must have figured he was saving this seat for her, fellow ethnic. As a regular commuter, she had a right to her place in front.

The bus went up the turnaround ramp and over a feeder ramp, this girl working away at opening her window—got it open when they passed the Hills Brothers factory, where the long, tall Hindu in the white turban and yellow gown stood quaffing his coffee. The smell of the roasting coffee made promises of comfort. Then they were on the bridge, not the bridge for suicides, and journeying through the dark. The eastbound traffic takes the bottom deck, which may as well be a tunnel. You can see lights between the railings and the top deck, and thereby identify the shores, the hills, islands, highways, the other bridge.

"Going to Oakland?" asked the girl. She said "Oak Lun."

"Haw," he grunted, a tough old China Man. If he were Japanese, he could have said, *"Ee, chotto."* Like "Thataway for a spell." Not impolite. None of your business, ma'am.

"I go to the city Fridays to work," she said. "Tuesdays and Thursdays, I'm taking a night course at Cal Extension, over by the metal overpass on Laguna Street. There's the bar and the traffic light on the corner? Nobody goes into or comes out of that bar. I stand there at that corner all by myself, obeying the traffic light. There aren't any cars. It's sort of lonely going to college. What do you go into the city for?" He didn't answer. Does she notice that he isn't the forthcoming, outgoing type? "On business, huh?" Suggesting an answer for him.

"Yeah. Business."

"I signed up for psychology," she said, as if he'd conversably asked. "But I looked up love in tables of contents and indexes, and do you know love isn't in psychology books? So I signed up for philosophy, but I'm getting disappointed. I thought we were going to learn about good and evil, human nature, how to be good. You know. What God is like. You know. How to live. But we're learning about 'P' plus 'Q' arrows 'R' or 'S.' What's that, haw? I work all day, and commute for two hours, and what do I get? 'P' plus 'Q' arrows 'R.' "

She ought to be interesting, going right to what's

important. The trouble with most people is that they don't think about the meaning of life. And here's this girl trying for heart truth. She may even have important new information. So how come she's boring? She's annoying him. Because she's presumptuous. Nosiness must be a Chinese racial trait. She was supposing, in the first place, that he was Chinese, and therefore, he has to hear her out. Care how she's getting along. She's reporting to him as to how one of our kind is faring. And she has a subtext: I am intelligent. I am educated. Why don't you ask me out? He took a side-eye look at her flat profile. She would look worse with her glasses off. Her mouse-brown hair was pulled tight against her head and up into a flat knot on top, hairpins showing, crisscrossing. (Do Jews look down on men who use bobby pins to hold their yarmulkes on?) A person has to have a perfect profile to wear her hair like that. She was wearing a short brownish jacket and her bony wrists stuck out of the sleeves. A thin, springtime skirt. She's poor. Loafers with striped socks. Flat shoes, flat chest, flat hair, flat face, flat color. A smell like hot restaurant air that blows into alleys must be coming off her. Char sui? Fire duck? Traveling with food, unto this generation. Yeah, the lot of us riding the Greyhound out of Fresno and Watsonville and Gardena and Lompoc to college—even Stanford—guys *named* Stanford—with mama food and grandma food in the overhead rack and under the seat. Pretending the smell was coming off somebody else's luggage. And here was this girl, a night school girl, a Continuing Ed girl, crossing the Bay, bringing a fire duck weekend treat from Big City Chinatown to her aging parents.

"Do you know my cousin Annette Ah Tye?" she asked. "She's from Oak Lun."

"No," he said.

"How about Susan Lew? Oh, come on, Susie Lew. Robert Lew, then. Do you know Fanny them? Fanny, Bobby, Chance Ong, Uncle Louis. I'm related to Fanny them."

"No, I don't know them," said Wittman, who would not be badgered into saying, "Oh, yeah, Susan them. I'm related by marriage to her cousin from Walnut Creek."

"I'm thinking of dropping philosophy," she said. "Or do you think the prof is working up to the best part?"

"I don't know what you say," Wittman. *Know* like *no*, like *brain*. "I major in engineer."

"Where do you study engineering?"

"Ha-ah." He made a noise like a Samurai doing a *me-ay*, or an old Chinese guy who smokes too much.

"You ought to develop yourself," she said. "Not only mentally but physically, spiritually, and socially." What nerve. Chinese have a lot of nerve. Going to extension classes was her college adventure.

To her, this was a modern young American student conversation. Let's use our intellectual college ideas. Let me be a real college girl talking smart. "You may be developing yourself mentally," she said. "But you know what's wrong with Chinese boys? All you do is study, but there's more to life than that. You need to be well-rounded. Go out for sports. Go out on dates. Those are just two suggestions. You have to think up other activities on your own. You can't go by rote and succeed, as in engineering school. You want a deep life, don't you? That's what's wrong with Chinese boys. Shallow lives."

What Wittman ought to say at this point was, "Just because none of us asks you out doesn't mean we don't go out with girls." Instead, to be kind, he said, "I not Chinese. I Japanese boy. I hate being taken for a chinaman. Now which of my features is it that you find peculiarly Chinese? Go on. I'm interested."

"Don't say chinaman," she said.

Oh, god. Oh, Central Casting. Who do you have for me now? And what is this role that is mine? Confederates who have an interest in race: the Ku Klux Klan, Lester Maddox, fraternity guys, Governor Faubus, Governor Wallace, Nazis—stupid people on his level. The dumb part of himself that eats Fritos and goes to movies was avidly interested in race, a topic unworthy of a great mind. Low karma shit. Baby talk. Stuck at A,B,C. Can't get to Q. Crybaby.

Race—a stupid soul-narrowing topic, like women's rights, like sociology, easy for low I.Q. people to feel like they're thinking. Stunted and runted at a low level of inquiry, stuck at worm. All right, then, his grade point average was low (because of doing too many life things), he's the only Chinese-American of his generation not in grad school, he'll shovel shit.

"It's the nose, is it, that's a chinaman nose?" he asked this flat-nosed girl. "Or my big *shinajin* eyes? Oh, I know. I know. Legs. You noticed my Chinese legs." He started to pull up a pants leg. "I'm lean in the calf. Most Japanese are meaty in the calf by nature, made for wading in rice paddies. Or it's just girls who have *daikon* legs? How about you? You got *daikon* legs?"

She was holding her skirt down, moving her legs aside, not much room among her packages. Giggling. Too bad she was not offended. Modern youth in flirtation. "You Japanese know how to have a social life much better than Chinese," she said. "At least you Japanese boys take your girls out. You have a social life."

Oh, come on. Don't say "your girls." Don't say "social life." Don't say "boys." Or "prof." Those Continuing Ed teachers are on a nontenure, non-promotional track. Below lecturers. Don't say "Chinese." Don't say "Japanese."

"You know why Chinese boys don't go out?" she

asked, confiding some more. Why? What's the punch-line? He ought to kill her with his bare hands, but waited to hear just why Chinese boys stay home studying and masturbating. You could hear her telling on us to some infatuated sinophile. Here it comes, the real skinny. "Because no matter how dumb-soo, every last short boy unable to get a date in high school or at a university can go to Hong Kong and bring back a beautiful woman. Chinese boys don't bother to learn how to socialize. It's not fair. Can you imagine a girl going to China looking for a husband? What would they say about her? Have you ever heard of a Japanese girl sending for a picture groom?"

"No," he said.

"And if Chinese boys don't learn to date, and there are millions of wives waiting to be picked out, then what becomes of girls like me, haw?"

Oh, no, never to be married but to a girl like this one. Montgomery Clift married to Shelley Winters in *A Place in the Sun*. Never Elizabeth Taylor.

"You shouldn't go to China to pick up a guy anyway," he said. "Don't truck with foreigners. They'll marry you for your American money and a green card. They'll say and do anything for a green card and money. Don't be fooled. They'll dump you once they get over here."

Another plan for her, or for anybody, might be to go to a country where your type is their ideal of physical beauty. For example, he himself could go to Scandinavia. But where would her type look good? Probably the U.S.A. is already her best bet. There's always white guys from Minnesota and Michigan looking for geisha girls.

"No, they won't," she said. "They'd be grateful. They're grateful and faithful forever. I'm not going to China. People can't just go to China. I was talking hypothetically." Oh, sure, she's so attractive.

"Last weekend, I went to a church dance," she said, letting him know she's with it. "I went with my girl friends. We go to dances without a date for to meet new boys. All the people who attended the dance were Chinese. How is that? I mean, it's not even an all-Chinese church. The same thing happens at college dances. Posters on campuses say 'Spring Formal,' but everyone knows it's a Chinese-only dance. How do they know? Okay, Chinese know. They know. But how does everybody else know not to come? Is it like that with Japanese?"

"I don't go to dances." Don't say "they."

"You ought to socialize. I guess the church gave the dance so we could meet one another. It's a church maneuver, see? To give us something beneficial. We'd come to their buildings for English lessons, dances, pot luck, and pretty soon, we're staying for the services. Anyway, there was a chaperone at this dance who was a white acquaintance of mine from high school. We're the same age, but he was acting like an adult supervisor of children. We used to talk with each other at school, but at this dance, of course, he wouldn't ask me to dance."

"What for you want to dance with him? Oh. Oh, I get it. I know you. I know who you are. You're Pocahontas. That's who you are. Aren't you? Pocahontas. I should have recognized you from your long crane neck."

"No, my name is Judy. Judy Louie." She didn't get it. She continued telling him more stuff about her life. On and on. Hadn't recognized her for a talker until too late. Strange moving lights, maybe airplanes, maybe satellites, were traveling through the air. The high stationary lights were warnings, the tops of hills. It seemed a long ride; this voice kept going on beside his ear. He looked at the girl again, and she looked blue-black in the dark. He blinked, and saw sitting beside him a blue boar. Yes, glints of light on bluish dagger tusks. Little shining eyes. Not an illusion, because the details were very sharp. Straight black bristly eyelashes. A trick of the dark? But it was lasting. Eyes and ivory tusks gleaming black and silver. Like black ocean with star plankton and black sky with stars. And the mouth moving, opening and closing in speech, and a blue-red tongue showing between silver teeth, and two ivory sword tusks. He leaned back in his seat, tried forward, and she remained a

blue boar. (You might make a joke about it, you
know. "Boar" and "bore.") He couldn't see where
her face left off from her hair and the dark. He made
no ado about his hallucination, acted as if she were a
normal girl. Concentrated hard to hear what she was
saying. "You're putting me on, aren't you?" she was
saying.

"What you mean?"

"You're not really Japanese. You're *Chi*nese. Japanese have good manners." Her piggy eyes squinted
at him. He wanted to touch her, but she would think
he was making a pass. But surely, he could try touching a tusk because the tusks can't actually be there.
"And you look Chinese. Big bones. Long face. Sort
of messy."

"Listen here. I'm not going to ask you out, so quit
hinting around, okay?"

"What? Me go out with you? I not hinting around.
I wouldn't go out with you if you ask me. You not
my type. Haw."

"What type is that? Missionaries? Missionaries your
type? You know where you ought to go for your
type? I know the place for you. In New York, there's
a nightclub for haoles and orientals to pick each other
up. It's like a gay bar, that is, not your average straight
thing. Sick. Girls such as yourself go there looking
for an all-American boy to assimilate with, and vice

versa. You can play Madame Butterfly or the Dragon Lady and find yourself a vet who's remembering Seoul or Pearl Harbor or Pusan or Occupied Japan. All kinds of Somerset Maugham combinations you hardly want to know about. Pseudo psycho lesbo Sappho weirdo hetero homo combos."

"You the one sick. Look who's sick. Don't call me sick. You sick." The blue boar had eyebrows, and they were screwed together in perplexity. "*If* you are Japanese, you shouldn't go out with a Chinese girl anyway, and I wouldn't go out with you. Japanese males work too hard. Chinese males dream too much, and fly off in the air. The Chinese female is down-to-earth, and makes her man work. When a Japanese man marries a Chinese woman, which does not happen often, it's tragic. They would never relax and have fun. A Japanese man needs a girl who will help him loosen up, and a Chinese man needs a girl who will help him settle down. Chinese man, Chinese woman, stay together. I'm going to do a study of that if I go into psych."

"Don't say 'tragic.' You want the address of that place where *keto hakujin* meet *shinajin* and *nihonjin*? Look, I'm just helping you out with your social life."

His talking to her, and her speaking, did not dispel her blueness or her boarness. The lips moved, the tusks flashed. He wanted her to talk some more to be able to look closely at her. What was causing this effect? The other people on the bus had not turned into animals.

"Help *yourself* out with your *own* social life. Why *don't* you ask me out on a date? Haw?" The boar lips parted smiling. "Because you are scared." "Sked," she pronounced it. "You been thinking about it this whole trip, but you sked." Don't say "date."

"No, I'm not." You're homely. That's the real reason. She's homely, and she doesn't know it. But he's not going to be the one to break the news to her.

This guise, though, is not plain. A magnificent creature. The voice that was coming out of it was the plain girl's. She must be sitting next to him engulfed in a mirage.

He touched her on a tusk, and it was there, all right. It did not fade into a strip of metal that was the window frame. The narrow eyes looked at him in surprise. "Hey, cut it out," she said, pushing his hand away from her mouth with a gentle cloven hoof. She giggled, and he backed away as far over by the aisle as he could back. What he had touched was harder than flesh. Bony. Solid. Therefore, real, huh? She giggled again. It is pretty funny to have somebody touching you on the teeth. Warm teeth.

"What was that for? Why did you do that?" she said. "Why you touch my teeth? That isn't the way to ask for a date."

"I'm not asking you for a date. I do not want to date you."

"Well, I understand. You don't like aggressive girls. Most guys can't take aggressive girls. I'm very aggressive." She'll never admit to homeliness. "Aggressive girls are especially bad for Japanese boys."

"Lay off my race," he said. "Cool it." Which was what he should have said in the first place. She went quiet. Sat there. But did not change back. The bus went on for a long time in the dark. And whenever he glanced her way, there beside him was the blue-black boar. Gleaming.

"Hey," he said, tapping her on the shoulder. That did feel like cloth, didn't it? Of course, he didn't know but that boar skin feels like corduroy. She cocked a flap of silky ear toward him. "See these people on the bus? They all look human, don't they? They look like humans but they're not."

"They are too," she said.

"Let me warn you." He looked behind him, and behind her. "Some of them only appear to be human." What he was saying even sent shivers up his own back. "There are nonhumans in disguise as men and women amongst us."

"Do you see them everywhere, or only on this bus?"

"On this bus, maybe a few other places. I'm surprised you haven't noticed. Well, some of them have gotten the disguise down very well. But there's usually a slip-up that gives them away. Do you want me to tell you some.signs to watch out for?"

The boar's great blue-black head nodded.

"You've seen *The Twilight Zone* on TV, haven't you? Have you noticed that Rod Serling doesn't have an upper lip?" He demonstrated, pressing his upper lip against his teeth. "That's a characteristic sign of the werewolf." The glittery eyes of the boar opened as wide as they could open. "Their hands are different from ours. They wear gloves. Walt Disney draws them accurately. And Walter Lantz does too. Goofy wears gloves, but not Pluto. Goofy is a dog, and Pluto is a dog, but Pluto is a real dog. Mickey and Minnie, Donald and the nephews, Unca Scrooge—and Yosemite Sam—never take their gloves off. Minnie and Daisy wash dishes with their gloves on. You see women in church with the same little white gloves, huh? They are often going to church. There are more of these werewomen in San Francisco than in other cities."

"What do they want? What are they doing here?"

"You tell me. I think they're here because they belong here. That's just the way the world is. There's all kinds. There are cataclysms and luck that they probably manipulate. But there's different kinds of them too, you know; they don't get along with one

another. It's not like they're all together in a con-
spiracy against our kind."

"Aiya-a-ah, nay gum sai nay, a-a-ah," said the creature beside him. *"Mo gum sai nay, la ma-a-ah."* Such
a kind voice, such a loving-kind voice, so soothing,
so sorry for him, telling him to let go of the old
superstitious ways.

She was not admitting to being weird.

At last, the bus shot out of the bridge-tunnel. Under
the streetlights, she turned back into a tan-and-gray
drab of a girl again. Wittman got himself to stand up,
rode standing up, and the bus reached the intersection
of Telegraph and Alcatraz. "Here's where I get off."

"Good-bye," she said. "Let's talk again. It will
make our commute more interesting."

He said, "Huh." Samurai.

What had that been about? Never mind. It's gone.
Forget it. It doesn't mean a thing. No miracle. No
miracles forevermore, because they may be drug
flashes. I've lost my miracles. It don't mean shit.

Oh no, the plain girl had gathered up her smelly
stuff, and gotten off behind him, and was following
him up the street. "Are you going to a party too?"
she asked. "Are we going to the same party?"

"No," he said. I'm not walking in with Miss Re-
freshment Committee bringing salt fish and rice, and
pork with *hom haw*. "No party," he said, and walked

off in the opposite direction of the way he was meaning to go. No more to do with you, girl. He walked
quickly ahead and away down Alcatraz. The group
of lights in the Bay must be the old federal pen. The
Rock. As usual, Orion the Warrior ruled the city sky,
and you had to know the Pleiades to find their nest.
He turned right, then right again, and up the hill to
the party.

COLONY

Rick Wernli

YEAR ONE

It was raining in Omaha.

Beyond the schoolroom window, the world was lost in a haze of gray shadows and darkness, a scene blurred and twisted by the rippling streaks of water that danced outside the glass. The droplets tapped incessantly against the pane, like something invisible seeking a way inside.

Mathew adjusted his glasses and turned to face the class. The children had gathered their chairs in a circle near the bookshelf, as they did every morning, and one of the girls was entertaining the group with a very impromptu rain dance. He smiled and checked his watch . . . let her dance.

As he closed the door he glanced into the hall and saw a yellow slicker peeking around the stairwell corner. He looked back at the other children and then walked across the corridor.

Sitting at the top of the stairs was a small boy with dark hair, his slicker still wet, the hood pulled back, the buttons undone. The teacher was surprised to find him crying.

"Hey, little buddy, what's wrong?" He sat next to the boy. "Want to tell me about it?"

The child tried to speak, but the words were only sobs, broken and meaningless.

"Take it easy." Mathew put his hand on the boy's shoulder. "It's okay."

Little arms clutched his waist, and the small face buried itself in his shoulder.

"Momma." The voice was weak. "They took my momma."

Another one?

Slowly his arms encircled the child, and his lips formed useless words.

"It's all right. I understand. Don't cry."

The boy sniffled and sighed, then grew quiet, but the tears went on flowing, soaking into the man's jacket.

"I'm sure your mother will be fine."

The child shook his head.

"Sure she will. They probably just want to ask her some questions or something."

"No . . . I heard Grandma on the phone. 'They'll kill her,' that's what she said. 'They'll kill her for writing that book.' "

"Maybe you didn't hear it right."

"She said they'd kill Momma, just like Poppa, 'cause she wrote bad stories."

"Your mother wrote about Colonists?" He almost knew without asking.

The boy nodded. "She hates them, more than Poppa did. She says they're monsters."

"There are no monsters."

The boy looked up, his eyes red. "Grandma says they're monsters, too."

"Colonists aren't monsters. They just aren't like us, that's all."

"But . . . are you sure?"

The teacher forced a smile. "Sure I'm sure. In fact, that's what we'll be talking about in class this morning. I have an idea. Why don't you sit next to me and be my assistant today. Would you like that?"

"Don't know." The boy shrugged. "Guess so."

"Good. Let's not keep everybody waiting, okay? We'll talk more later."

"Okay."

The boy set his rain gear aside at the door and then joined the other children in the circle of chairs.

"Who knows what day it is?" Mathew prompted.

"April!" someone shouted, and the others laughed.

"April is close. It's Friday, April tenth, and that means one year ago the Colonists came to Earth. Who can tell us how they got here?"

"The spaceship!" several children yelled at once.

"That's right, a big, gray spaceship, shaped like . . . ?"

"An egg!"

"Right. And where is this spaceship?"

"New York City!"

"Good. And what's it doing there?"

Blank faces.

"You're right. It's not really doing anything, is it? It's just floating in the air over the United Nations Building. Who knows where the spaceship came from?"

Again, silence.

"Right. Nobody knows where the Colonists come from, because they haven't told us yet. There's an awful lot about these space travelers we just don't understand, but we're learning all the time, and today I want to tell you about some of the really interesting things we do know."

The teacher turned to the boy at his side. "Mister Assistant, would you show us where China is?"

The child hurried from his seat to stand before the wall map, pointing to a large, red splotch.

"Very good."

Wearing a fragile smile, the boy resumed his seat.

"China is very far away from here. That's where the Colonists decided to make their home on our planet. They call it 'Colony,' and it's made of domes, lots of domes all connected, like a big bunch of bubbles. They live inside these bubbles, because they can't breathe regular air like we do."

There were noises outside the window, vague motions beyond the glass, traffic, activity, voices.

"Uh, the air they need to breathe is called 'methane,' and they fill up those bubbles with it."

The noise came closer, moving up the stairway and into the hall—footsteps, movement, angry protests.

"The Colonists are very different from us. . . ."

The sound of a scuffle came from beyond the door.

"I'll just go see what's happening outside," he said, but he was barely out of his seat when the door suddenly swung open.

Across the threshold strode a woman in gray uniform with a United Nations emblem at the lapel. She wore a Colonial radiocom on her belt and a holstered automatic at her side. Behind her, men and women were leading children from other classrooms toward the stairs as several uniformed guards stood watch.

The teacher just stood there, staring.

"My name is Captain Ryan," the woman told him. "I have orders from the secretary general to evacuate the premises. You will escort your class down to the bus lines in an orderly fashion, beginning immediately."

"I will not! What is all this!? I was never informed . . ."

"No one was informed, sir. I have my orders."

"To hell with your orders! Where's the principal?"

"She's receiving medical attention at the moment. I would advise you not to interfere." The woman unsnapped the holster with gloved fingers. "Clear?"

"You can't do this!"

"I have a Colonial directive that says otherwise, and that's all the authority I need. Now lead these children downstairs."

"No . . ." Mathew swallowed nervously. "I refuse."

"Very well."

Two men in uniform entered at the captain's signal.

"All right, children." She smiled. "We're all going on a nice bus ride."

The men moved among the students, herding them toward the door, and the children were too frightened to resist.

"Where are you taking them?"

"Manhattan," the woman replied. "Special housing has been provided . . ."

"New York! But the parents—"

"Parental consent is not required."

The uniformed men paused at the door to let the children don their rain gear.

"What's this all about? Why are you doing this?"

"You'll get your evacuation instructions on the broadcast networks tonight," the Captain replied.

"This area's been selected as the next site for Colony construction. Everything within twenty miles of here—"

"Next site!? What are you talking about?"

"The secretary was informed last night. More Colonists are coming. The seedship was just the beginning. Colony will be expanded."

"But . . . I don't understand what this has to do with the children!"

"It's for their own good," the woman assured him. "They'll be just fine. Better off, in fact."

"What do you mean?"

"It's not something I'm at liberty to discuss."

"Gene fixing! That's it, isn't it? I've heard stories—"

"You shouldn't listen to idle talk."

"But they're just children!"

"The technique only works on children. Don't be so concerned. We're extending their lives."

Suddenly the boy in the yellow slicker ran from the line and threw his arms around the teacher.

"Don't let them take me!" he cried. "Please!"

They both struggled to hold on as men in gray uniforms pried them apart, one wrapping Mathew in a headlock as the other dragged the child, kicking and screaming, from the room.

"Please!" the boy yelled, and then he was gone.

The teacher stumbled forward as the arm around

his throat released him, and his glasses fell to the floor.
He moved quickly for the door, but the captain's
drawn revolver stopped him.

"Don't."

He could only stand by and watch as the last few
children were taken from the room.

"Be sensible," the woman said, holstering her
weapon. "There's nothing you can do. There's nothing anyone can do."

"We could try."

She shook her head, then turned and started for the
door.

"I was wrong," Mathew said softly.

"What?"

"They are monsters." His eyes were dark and cold.
"And so are we."

YEAR ONE HUNDRED

There was a parade.

High on the rooftops, the children looked up in wonder, as many had a century before, but it was not the great seedship that held their interest on this day. Featureless, motionless, the huge gray ovoid hung effortlessly above the city, just as it had for one hundred years. It was now too commonplace to be an object of curiosity, even for children.

It was the parade they awaited. Public ceremonies were always amusing, and this promised to be an event without parallel. "Be part of the greatest celebration in history!" declared the broadcast networks. "The Great Centennial of Colony Earth is upon us! Be happy!" So the children were ready. A parade, after all, was a good reason to party.

At the center of the main group, a small boy with long, dark hair moved slowly from child to child selling small tabs of micro, each shaped like a smooth, gray egg. He slid gracefully across the rooftop on silent airskates, pausing once to drink from an offered flask of brandywine, then moving on to distribute his wares. Between sales, he occasionally glanced up at the oncoming parade.

Amid the distant sound of music and cheering crowds, thousands of wind-borne vessels approached in wide formation. Floats and flyers and balloons of every description filled the horizon, all trailing banners and plumes of colored smoke. Kites and gliders circled the smaller floats, rising and swooping in daring patterns to excite and amaze, while the large balloons carried tails of prismwire to dazzle the eye.

Reaching the fringe of the group, the boy paused before turning back, surprised to find a girl sitting alone at the roof's edge, her feet dangling over the precipice. She showed no interest in the parade, her eyes downcast. He considered her a moment, wary of her mood, then shrugged and smiled. "Why not?"

She looked up as he drew nearer, then turned away, pretending not to notice him.

"Day." He smiled, sitting beside her.

"Day," she replied, still looking away.

"Can't see the parade too well from here." He strained his neck to gaze over the heads of children standing behind them.

"Hadn't noticed." The girl frowned.

"See real good over there," he noted, pointing to the front of the group.

"So, go over there," she said, and her eyes turned their pain and anger at him.

"Intend to, don't worry. Just thought you might need chemistry."

She stared at the small gray pill in his outstretched hand, then shook her head. "Not today."

"Why not?" the boy asked, gesturing toward the

parade with a sweep of his arm. "New Year's Day, right?"

The children nearby began to cheer as the music grew louder. It was Colony music, but perfomed live by humans with real Earth instruments. The parade was getting close.

"Good reason to party," he reminded her, hoping to raise her spirits. "Hundred-year anniversary, know?"

"Really been a hundred years?" She sighed. Her eyes were damp as she glanced up at the Colony ship overhead. "That long?"

Confused, but sympathetic, the boy followed her gaze.

"Should be happy," he said softly. "Should be grateful. Nobody gets sick. Nobody grows old. Nobody goes hungry. Hundred years of peace and plenty. Hundred years today. Something special."

The girl turned to watch as the leading edge of the procession moved overhead, but she seemed unimpressed and quickly lost interest. Gazing down into the street, she followed the shadows of the parade crawling across the pavement far below.

"Lots of progress, know?" he encouraged. "New treaty, new trade laws . . . more metals, better technology, new drugs . . . and more freedom, too. . . ."

"Yo." She nodded. "More freedom. Free to work

in Colony factories, free to build Colony machines, free to do Colony labor. . . . Freedom to be servants."

The cheering grew louder, and the boy looked to see the larger floats rising above the crowd, moving slowly overhead. The music reached a peak as streamers were launched over the rooftops, and the children cried out with surprise. The girl hesitated, then turned to look.

Someone was pointing to the first of the large floats as it came near, and soon the entire gathering was following its passage, observing its passenger with wonder.

"It's Cavernstone Blue!" someone yelled.

Straining his eyes to stare into the protective bubble at the prow of the float, the boy caught a glimpse of the alien within its murky green atmosphere.

"Hey!" he shouted. "It is!"

The girl turned to him, suddenly curious.

"What is?"

"Cavernstone Blue." The boy smiled. "That's its name in English, anyway. First Colonist to fly solo from Homeworld to Earth! Just in time for Year One Hundred, too!"

Looking up again, the girl glared at the thing within its weapon-proof shield. When it raised itself on four stalks and shook its topmost stems, it seemed to be waving to the crowd.

"Colonists not all bad," the boy argued. "Cleaned up the air and water, solved the population problem, gave us weather control, solar power, space travel . . ."

The girl began to laugh, a sad, hollow laugh that startled him.

"Cleaned up the world by supressing technology. Reduced population by killing resisters. Gave us nothing but demands. Can humans control weather, use solar power, travel in space? Can't even leave this city without permission, know?"

"But there's so much to learn," he countered. "Colonist technology is—"

"—is Colonist technology. Think humans will ever build starships? Powerpods? Warp-radio? Laser-cannon? Think Colonists will teach us that? All Colonists teach is slavery."

The boy said nothing, troubled to find his opinions so easily dismissed.

"Wanted to write something yesterday," the girl said quietly, almost talking to herself. "Wanted to see my thoughts on paper. . . . Ha! No one has paper! Aren't any trees! Aren't any plants or animals! Colonists changed the whole world to build Colony! Even took away our moon!"

Unable to answer, the boy gazed up at the flying procession that now filled half the sky. Directly overhead, children riding the larger floats were waving and throwing sparklers down to the rooftops. The

crowd cheered and waved back, tossing lightning
flares to show their approval, and everyone everywhere was smiling . . . except the girl.

"Not fair," she sighed. "Our planet, know?"

Trying to ignore her, he closed his eyes and let the
spirit of celebration grow inside him again. Everything she told him was true. He knew it. But there
was nothing to be done about it. Nothing to do at
all, except party. Life was just one long search for
reasons to party. Feeling better, he turned to face the
girl with renewed enthusiasm, anxious to share his
thoughts.

Then he realized she was gone.

He glanced about the rooftop quickly with a growing sense of panic, knowing he would not find her
there. Reaching into his pocket he grabbed a tab of
micro and swallowed it quickly. His hands were shaking as he moved away from the precipice, determined
not to look down.

The drug kicked in quickly, and in moments he
was calm again.

Soon he decided there was no reason for concern.

There was only a reason to party.

There was a parade.

YEAR ONE THOUSAND

It was a glorious day on Colony K'Mirra.

Rose-colored clouds drifted lazily across a burgundy sky, and the small amber suns turned slowly in their closely coupled dance as they wandered nearer to zenith. The winds were from the west, calm and cool, scented with sea-borne flowers and ocean spray, and only the soft, lulling songs of predatory birds disturbed the morning's peace.

Moving like a wraith above the landscape, a small boy with long, dark hair rode a silent airsled over the meadows to the very edge of native territory. With great skill and care the rider steadily slowed the floating disc, until the vehicle was finally brought to rest on a large patch of orange moss not far from the border. A few steps away, the vibrant colors of the meadowmoss ended abruptly, and beyond lay only dark-gray, sterile ground, creating a line that marked with perfect accuracy the outermost perimeter of Colony, where nothing native was permitted to grow.

Leaving the airsled unguarded, the boy slipped a small backpack onto his shoulders, prepared to walk the remaining distance. He paused before crossing the deadline, then marched rapidly onto the barren plain of ash and dust, leaving a long trail of small gray clouds in his wake.

The core structure rose from the devastated land

like a great frozen froth, a vast network of interlocking domes filled with the murky green air of Homeworld, and at the base of the nearest dome, a gently tiered abutment formed a curving stairway of wide metal steps.

When he finally reached the structure's edge, the boy checked the chronometer on his wrist, then ascended the stairs quickly, stepping up onto a wide ledge that circled the entire complex. A single portal opened in the side of the structure, and the youth entered without hesitation, moving through a dark corridor to a transparent, bubblelike chamber within the dome's interior.

The lights of the reception area grew brighter as the visitor entered, and the voice of the Colony regent was heard on the speech simulator almost at once.

"You have not been summoned."

The boy waited, standing alone inside a small pocket of native air, gazing into the thick, green, alien atmosphere that surrounded him. After a long silence he saw the tall, bushy figure of the regent begin to take shape in the mist, growing larger and larger as it moved across the dome, until it stood beside the transparent airlock, towering over the human occupant.

"Respond."

"Something happened."

The regent leaned forward, its optical fronds focused on the youth, studying his face, his posture, but there was nothing about his appearance that seemed unusual.

"Explain."

The boy paused, then spoke in a strangely solemn tone.

"I have to go home."

The Colonist shook its petals in confusion. "That response is inadequate."

"True," the human sighed.

"You were assigned to assist the Colony engineer. Explain your presence here."

"Demolition was scheduled today."

The regent consulted its total recall to confirm the information. "A scaled tectonic macroblast will occur at Site Two within—"

"Demolition cannot occur as planned."

Long stems whipped the gloomy air in a show of displeasure. "Explain!"

"Still furballs on the island."

The Colonist appeared to relax as it lowered itself onto eight stalks.

"The animal life forms you term 'furballs' have been rated sentient at the same level of perception as humans. Evacuation instructions were issued on the broadcast networks in all native languages—"

"Some furballs understand, but still refuse to leave."

"Then those creatures that remain will be destroyed."

"Detonation could be postponed—"

"Delay is impractical," the regent countered. Then its manner turned skeptical. "Explain your concerns in this matter. You were employed on Earthlike worlds before. You terminated many life forms in the service of Colony. Perhaps your reluctance grows from their similarity to humans."

"Furballs?" the boy objected. "Look more like otters than people."

"They are animal. You are animal. Consider how this affects your judgment."

"Well . . ." The human bowed his head. "Suppose so."

The Colonist twirled its stamen in a show of satisfaction. "It is well you admit it."

"Their eyes," the boy explained. "Like human eyes . . ."

"Such emotional responses are common among animals. Perhaps you should be reassigned."

"Please, try to understand," the youth replied, his voice weak and tired. "I have to go home."

"Permission to return to the Colony of origin," the regent answered, "is not a valid request."

The boy glanced up, his young face strangely aged. "Know what today is?"

The Colonist remained silent, uncertain, but the human went on without waiting for reply.

"New Year's Day," he announced, "Year One Thousand."

The regent checked its memory. "You refer to time scales and customs associated with your planet of origin; an anniversary celebrating colonization."

"Thousand years today." The boy nodded. "Calculated the date myself."

"Explain the relevance."

"Met a girl on New Year's Day in the year One Hundred." As he spoke, his voice began to fade. "Tried to forget her. Such a long time ago, but I still remember the way she looked, the sound of her voice . . ."

"There is no apparent relevance."

"Her eyes," the boy sighed. "Never will forget her eyes."

"Be warned. Your response is perceived as irrational. Failure to provide the proper response to—"

"Don't know the proper response!" the youth shouted. "Don't know how to make you understand! Can't do this anymore! I have to go home!"

"You are from Colony Earth," the Regent reminded him.

"Yo."

"That Colony is fully established. The entire planet

was terraformed to Homeworld standard. You would find the air unbreathable, the temperature unbearable; you could not even survive without life support. The world you knew no longer exists."

The boy lowered his eyes and spoke in a whisper. "I know."

"You are a Colonial subject. You serve on the planet you are assigned. There is nowhere else for you to go."

The boy checked his chronometer again. Then he slipped the backpack from his shoulders and removed a small black cylinder.

"This is yours," he said. "Came to give it back."

The regent recognized the device at once, and the speech simulator conveyed a sense of alarm. "A fusion cap!"

"Took it from Site Two this morning."

"Site . . . Two . . ." the regent said, rigid with fear.

"Had to plant the engineer to get it."

There was unmistakable terror in the artificial voice. "Irrational!! Irrational!! Detonation imminent!!"

"Tried to explain," the boy said. "I have to go home."

He held the warhead gently in his palms, watching the timer count down the last few digits.

"And I'm taking you with me."

ABOUT THE CONTRIBUTING
AUTHORS

ANA CASTILLO received one of the first fiction awards granted by the California Arts Council. She is the author of *Sapagonia*, a novel. Her story about a Hispanic family is evocative of her Chicano background.

GERALD HASLAM has written several short story collections, including *Okies and Snapshots*, and is the recipient of a California Arts Council fellowship for fiction.

JEANNE WAKATSUKI HOUSTON spent four years of her childhood at Manzanar, an internment camp for Japanese Americans during World War II. Her screenplay *Farewell to Manzanar*, based on her book of the same title, won a Humanitas Prize and a Christopher Award.

National Book Award winner MAXINE HONG KINGSTON is the author of *The Woman Warrior*, *China Men*, *Hawaii One Summer*, and *Tripmaster Monkey: His Fake Book*.

KEVIN KYUNG was born in Korea and lived on Guam for ten years before immigrating to the United States, where he now lives and works as a writer and teacher.

East Coast writer LOIS LOWRY is the author of many books for young people, including *A Summer to Die; Find a Stranger, Say Goodbye;* and *Anastasia Krupnik*. The author is the recipient of a Boston Globe Award and received the Newbery medal for *Number the Stars*.

GARY SOTO's story about first love is set in the Spanish-speaking neighborhood of his childhood. He has been awarded a Guggenheim Fellowship and an NEA Creative Writing Fellowship.

JOYCE CAROL THOMAS won the National Book Award and the American Book Award for *Marked by Fire;* her other novels include *Bright Shadow, Water Girl, The Golden Pasture,* and *Journey*. Ms. Thomas was born in Oklahoma, where as a girl she attended a black-American church a little like the one in her story.

GERALD VIZENOR, a mixed-blood member of the Minnesota Chippewa Tribe, won the Fiction Collective Prize and the Before Columbus American Book Award for his second novel, *Griever: An American Monkey King in China*.

New Jersey–born RICK WERNLI received a University of California Regents fellowship for creative writing. He is currently at work on his first novel.

AL YOUNG grew up in Mississippi and Detroit. He is the recipient of a Joseph Henry Jackson Award and a Stegner Writing Fellowship. His many novels include *Sitting Pretty* and *Seduction by Light*. His story of young black-American males could have taken place in his own Detroit neighborhood.